NIGHT WATCH

ARCANE SOULS WORLD

SOUL READER SERIES BOOK ONE

ANNIE ANDERSON

NIGHT WATCH

ARCANE SOULS WORLD

Soul Reader Series Book 1

International Bestselling Author

Annie Anderson

Edited by Angela Sanders

Cover Design by Tattered Quill Designs

www.annieande.com

For those that need a little bit of vengeance. This is for you.

Priestess of Storms & Stone

Queen of Fate & Fire

PHOENIX RISING SERIES

(Formerly the Ashes to Ashes Series)

Flame Kissed

Death Kissed

Fate Kissed

Shade Kissed

Sight Kissed

ROMANTIC SUSPENSE NOVELS

SHELTER ME SERIES

Seeking Sanctuary

Reaching Refuge

"Sooner or later, everyone sits down to a banquet of consequences."

— ROBERT LOUIS STEVENSON

Waking up in the middle of a cemetery was never high on my bucket list—not that I had a bucket list at twenty-two—but if I had one at all, hanging out in a graveyard wasn't *ever* going to be on it.

Of all the things that could have woken me up, it was the grainy yet damp sensation of dirt on my hands that did the trick.

Not the rain pelting me. Not the lash of wind chilling me to the bone. Not the fact that I was outside when I should be warm in my bed. No, those kernels of awareness came later. It was those simple granules of earth on my fingertips.

My first thought before I took in the world around me was, *Mom's gonna be pissed.* Yes, even being a twenty-two-year-old college senior, I gave a shit what my mommy thought. Especially when my mother was the reigning queen of finding me asleep in my bed with a spent charcoal in my hand and losing her freaking mind. To my credit, I hadn't been the one who decided I should live at home while I went to college. Nor had I been the one who'd insisted on crisp white sheets for a person who was perpetually covered in the remnants of whatever art medium she'd used that day.

Nope, that was on her.

Aching and groggy, it took a full minute to understand that I was, A—outside, and B—in the middle of a cemetery. At night. In a damp, nearly see-through nightgown that had never once graced my wardrobe.

Seemed legit.

Honestly, if I weren't in so much pain—if my gut wasn't roiling with hunger and my head wasn't feeling like someone had taken a pickax to it, I could've sworn I was dreaming. Well, not dreaming exactly. Having a nightmare would be more like it. I mean, why else would I be covered in dirt, sitting on the freshly dug mound of a grave?

It took a hell of a lot of concentration to read the headstone, but I wasn't at all surprised to read my own name: Sloane Emerson Cabot, with my birth and death date right underneath it.

As nightmares went, this was pretty solid. Too bad I had the sneaking suspicion I was in no way dreaming. After what seemed like ages, I moved, struggling to stand on unsteady legs. I stumbled, tripping over my own feet as I plopped back down on the loose earth of another freshly dug grave. I didn't want to look at the headstone, but it was hard to miss. It was double-sized, the granite slab meant for a couple.

The cold finally touched me then. The rain lashed at my face, the pain smashing into me in a wave so vast it threatened to pull me under as I read the names etched into the stone.

Rosalind and Peter Cabot. Right underneath their names was a death date that matched mine.

I heaved, even though my stomach was empty and had been for what felt like a year. When it finally calmed down, I stood again, wobbled, but managed to stay vertical long enough to recognize the cemetery. I passed it every day on my way to school. Whispering Pines Cemetery was three blocks away from my house. In the opposite direction, closer to campus, was the police station.

Dithering, freezing, and hungrier than I'd ever been in my life, I fought with myself.

Should I go see if this was all a bad dream and hope my parents were sitting in their favorite chairs in our living room? Or did I go with my gut, knowing this wasn't fake or a dream or some elaborate prank? Did I go to the police—the only people I could think of who might be able to help me understand this mess?

You could go to Aunt Julie.

That thought streaked across my brain, like a flare in the darkness. Aunt Julie wasn't my aunt, but my mother's best friend. She might know what happened. But Julie was on the other side of town, not two blocks down the street. Cops first. They could call Aunt Julie. They could tell me if this was all one big joke.

Or they could lock you up in an insane asylum. That was an option, too.

No. Someone had done something to me. Someone had hurt me—hurt us. The police would help. They would call Aunt Julie. They would straighten this whole mess out. Or I'd wake up. That was still on the table.

My stomach wrenched, the pain so acute, I stumbled to my knees again. But I had a purpose. I had a place to go and a job to do. So, I got up, pointed my feet to the station, and put one foot in front of the other until I was moving.

My first obstacle was a chained gate, the arched metal moving with the wind. It screeched back and forth, almost like it was laughing at me. I grabbed the padlock, the bulky metal unyielding in my hand one second, and then cracking and breaking into little bits the next. It was true that I might have had a minor hissy fit when I saw the chained and padlocked wrought-iron gate. But my temper tantrum broke the likely rusted-out lock, and I pushed the stupidly heavy gate open. The hinges squealed even more, loud enough to wake the dead. At that thought, I started cackling like I had lost the very last bit of my mind.

But soon, laughing hurt my ribs, and my stomach pitched once more, causing me to catch myself on the trunk of a young poplar tree before I went down again. I stumbled toward my goal—the stone-faced municipal building that was half-jail and half-police station, the courthouse right across the street.

One foot in front of the other, Sloane. Keep moving.

For some reason, I heard that in my mother's voice. It reminded me of all the family hikes we'd gone on, the ones that we seemed to turn into a competitive sport with me losing every single time. Who thought ruck marches in the mountains for time was a family bonding moment? My parents, that's who.

Don't look back, sweet girl. Only forward.

The streetlight was my beacon in the darkness—all I had to do was follow my mother's words, and I'd be okay. It would all be okay. I trudged along, deciding to take a shortcut through the alley instead of following the sidewalk around the block when I retched on the pavement.

The contents of my stomach were a dark viscous liquid that smelled heavily of pennies. I didn't look too hard at what came up, but I didn't have a whole lot of time. I didn't feel so hot.

The brick walls of the alley buffeted the wind and a bit of the rain that seemed to want to lash sideways at me. The shivers didn't rattle my bones so hard, and at that tiny bit of relief, I wanted to curl up in the filth of the neglected lane and fall asleep. But, I only had a little bit farther to go.

Keep going, girl.

I heard the man before I saw him. Smelled him, too. But I was too busy staring at the blue and white Whispering Pines Police Department sign that kept me moving to really realize what the back of my brain was trying to tell me.

My hindbrain was screaming "Danger!" while my stupid front brain only thought about a cheeseburger and a bed and finding my parents. Still, I didn't see him until he was damn near on top of me—the burn of liquor on his breath making me gag. His hands were pale, like the thin fingers of death under his billowing sweatshirt and thick jacket. His face was mostly obscured by the hood, so I didn't catch the red to his eyes or length of his fangs until he'd shoved me against the bricks, their rough exterior digging into my shoulders.

I kicked—my only option since my wrists were caught in his long-fingered grip. He squeezed so hard the bones ground together—but my feeble attempts to injure him were met with a chuckle, eerie enough to keep me up at night.

"You think a fledgling is going to stop me? *Pfft*." His scoff was punctuated by a resounding crack across my face before he yanked my wrists over my head and pulled me up, my feet dangling above the ground. "Your maker should have told you to stay out of another vampire's territory. *Tsk, tsk, tsk*. I suppose I'll just have to send them a message. Your dead body should do just fine."

None of his words made much sense other than "dead body." Those I got loud and clear.

The rest? Not so much.

My stomach took that particular moment to wrench as if someone was reaching into my middle and yanking it out. Given the red-eyed man was currently licking his chops, I had to look down to make sure my flesh was still intact. Without a better option, I brought my knee up, catching him in the middle. He dropped me with a pained "oof!" and I fell to the dirty street. Only then did

I rake my hand across his face, my pitiful nails not hurting him too much, but drawing blood all the same.

"You little shit," he growled, backhanding me—knocking me back into the rough bricks. But I barely felt the pain of his blow.

No, I was too focused on the heavenly scent coming from his skin. It smelled like the juiciest steak, and my hunger rose, punching me so hard I felt my mouth water and my gut twist. Before I could fully comprehend what was happening, my teeth were in his throat.

Not at. *In.*

They had punched through his flesh while my body wrapped around him like a barnacle—latching onto anything that would keep the dark, blissfully tangy liquid running down my throat. It was like life was flowing into me, and it was all I could do to keep it.

All at once, images flooded my brain. Flashes of scenes no one wanted to see. Like the man—Jacob was his name—stealing the innocence of a girl who regrettably crossed his path. Or when he snapped the neck of an elderly bespectacled man in a tweed jacket who only asked him for the time. Or a mother and her baby...

Jacob had lived a very long time, and all the while, he'd hurt every single human who'd been unlucky enough to have been in his general vicinity. He hated humans. He hated everyone, and he meted out that hate at any and every opportunity.

I barely felt it when he fell to his knees, or when his ancient heart stopped beating. I drank and drank until there was nothing left. And then I tried to drink a little more. The pair of us were crumpled in the filth of that alley, and I didn't care one bit. All I wanted—no, *needed* —was more of that delicious liquid. My teeth were buried in Jacob's throat, even though there was nothing left of him to take.

Still, I hungered. And still, I took.

I couldn't say for sure when I knew I was consuming his soul—when I knew I was taking everything that he was—to satiate my need. It was definitely during the act itself, but I couldn't say how I knew. But only after I'd consumed the very last bit of his life force, did I fully realize what I'd done.

How I'd changed.

What I had become.

Shakily, I stood—staring down at the blood-soaked nightgown and the filth on my feet and the withered husk of Jacob's body that was quickly crumbling to ash.

Jacob had been a monster, and now, so was I.

My gaze slowly rose to the blue and white sign, that just a few minutes ago, was a beacon in the night, a place to seek refuge. Now it was nothing but a glaring reminder of what I had just done.

I couldn't go to the police. I couldn't go to Aunt Julie. Not if I could do to her what I'd done to him.

All I knew for sure was there was a grave in Whispering Pines Cemetery with my name on it.

Maybe it would be a good idea to just stay dead.

2

ONE YEAR LATER

The benefits of being dead very rarely made up for the whole "not being alive" bit of the utter shitshow I now called my existence. Well, I couldn't say for sure if I was dead or not. My heart still beat, my hair grew. I ate food… sometimes. I used the facilities when I needed them.

Okay, so the eating thing didn't happen as often as it used to. But I didn't burn in the sun and holy water didn't sting. *I'd checked.*

Yeah, I drank blood, and I'd be grossed out for sure if it didn't taste so damn good. But that was a precursor to the real meal—the soul eating part. Not that they were particularly scrumptious, but they were filling, that was for sure.

Taking the life and soul of the vampire who'd

attacked me had been what brought me here, and honestly, if it hadn't been for him, I wouldn't be able to kill the fuckers who harmed innocent people. Wouldn't be able to get their asses off the streets before they could kill or hurt someone else. That was the only thing I liked about this life—watching bad guys get what was coming to them.

It certainly wasn't the benefits or pay.

Since that fateful night, I made a habit of combing the streets of Ascension, searching for men like Jacob. Over the last year I'd chowed down on many a soul. To my credit, I only ate bad people, and if what I saw when I drank their blood was anything to go by, well... I was doing the world a favor. I'd get a meal, the world would be safer, and I'd feel a little better about my place in it. Which was why I was planning on planting the rapidly desiccating corpse in my truck in the same cemetery where I'd woken up a year ago.

I couldn't say for certain why I frequented the place. There were plenty of uninhabited woods in this part of the country. Plenty of hills that hadn't seen a soul in about fifty years. I could've buried this guy in one of them, but I didn't.

Now, that wasn't to say that all the people I'd consumed were vampires like Jacob. Not all of them were even a little bit supernatural. Or what was it they called themselves again? *A member of the Arcane world.*

Like that wasn't a mouthful.

Every now and again, I would throw a human into rotation if I caught them doing something they shouldn't. Like attacking women, beating children—that kind of thing. There was one guy who'd kicked a puppy into a wall. I made that guy wet himself before I drank him down.

Truth be told, I wasn't sorry for the lives I'd taken. That probably made me a horrible person, but as a newly formed villain, I just didn't give a shit.

My first order of business after taking Jacob's soul had been to pilfer his ash-laden clothes for his wallet. I'd gleaned enough from his memories to know he only kept cash and had a place in Ascension, a city on the other side of Whispering Pines. Ascension was big—bigger than the college town I'd grown up in—and there I started over, in a way. If one could call squatting starting over.

I had a good reason for being in Whispering Pines on this wretched evening, despite the smell of snow on the air and the bite to the wind. Said reason was currently rotting in the back of my truck, and it was going to take a bottle of Johnny Walker Blue Label, and at a minimum, two bills to get old Gerry to keep quiet about this.

Unlike when Jacob's body crumbled to ash, this body was too new, too fresh to give me the easy way out. My best guess—and about all I had was guesswork—was the younger the person, the fresher the body, the slower the decomp. Jacob, my first soul, had been nearly six hundred years old.

This one, not so much.

To my credit, the human I'd just snuffed out was the literal worst, and if I'd still been human, I would have seriously considered putting a bullet in his brain. Alas, I was not human, and Jeffery Carver Kingston III deserved it. If I could have resurrected him and killed him twice, I would have, but I wasn't that lucky. As it was, I'd have to be careful. Old Jeff here had a family with more money than scruples, and they'd be wondering where he'd gone if I didn't get him planted soon. Not that much could be done if the trail led the cops to a dead woman.

I swiped the expensive booze and hauled myself out of the truck. It wasn't mine, exactly, but I'd confiscated it from a rather unsavory gentleman after he'd been a snack. Finders, keepers, and all that. I'd have to give it up soon enough.

I minced my way around divots in the turf as I crushed over the dying grass to the groundkeeper's office. Gerry Ainsworth was an old, decrepit drunk with exactly zero interest in my comings and goings. After I paid him handsomely with booze and money, he paid me no never mind about what I did with his backhoe.

Usually.

The echo of a game show bounced through the hallway as I made my way to Gerry's office. The old man was just about the only person I talked to nowadays. I couldn't say we were on good terms, exactly, but he didn't ask too many questions.

Except for tonight.

I hadn't even been in the room two seconds—and he hadn't bothered to take his eyes off the screen—before he started in on me.

"You some kind of assassin or something?" he rasped, his voice gravelly, either from his smoking habit, his whiskey habit, or a combination of the two.

A chuckle bubbled its way up my throat. "Or something. I've come bearing gifts."

I met Gerry not long after I woke up at the foot of my own grave. Covered in blood, eyes glowing, and wearing a dead man's hoodie, Gerry had said I looked like a nightmare. Not much surprised the old man, and at sixty-seven, he'd informed me I wasn't the first dead thing to cross his path.

All in all, the conversation was less than comforting, but Gerry didn't call the cops and we'd set up a little bargain. Plus, he was the only person I could really go to when the bodies started piling up.

Gerry peeled his gaze from his show. "What have ya got for me?"

I showed him the box, enjoying when his eyes lit up when he saw the label. His smile was practically beatific when I slapped three hundred-dollar bills on his desk before gently placing the booze on top.

"Keys, please." He didn't reach for the drawer, which I knew held the keys to the backhoe. Gerry and I weren't too big on conversation, so his hesitation was more than a little worrisome.

As strong as I was, I had no interest in digging a grave by hand. No, thank you.

His gaze slid to the left, not quite looking away but also not meeting my eyes. "These people you kill, they're bad, right?"

Coy. I would go with coy. "Who says I kill people, Gerry? Maybe I just like digging in the dirt."

He sat back in his chair, the support brace creaking like it would snap at any second. "I figure, they have to be bad. 'Cause if they weren't, you probably would have killed me by now."

I snickered. "Yes, Gerry, if I were a serial killer, I probably would have killed you by now. But then again, I'd have to find my own backhoe, and those aren't cheap." I held out my hand, uneasiness hitting me square in the chest when he flinched. "Keys?"

"You can't keep doing this, Sloane," he whispered, and if I didn't have such good hearing, I probably wouldn't have caught the fear in his voice. "Someone is going to notice. There's already talk of a vigilante out killing people."

Funny, I hadn't read a word about a vigilante in any local news article. Not at all. And I'd been watching, too.

At my confused expression, he chuckled. "Not in the human news, kid. But the arcane world is small. Big fish go missing? People talk. Someone is going to connect the dots right back to you if you don't cool it."

Doubtful. Real freaking doubtful.

"I hear you."

Gerry gave me a mirthless laugh. "Sure you do, kid." He slapped the keys in my hand. "This is the last time, Sloane. You got me?"

"Fine," I growled, letting a little peek of my other side leak into my eyes. If Gerry knew how this had all gotten started, he might have been a little more sympathetic. Then again, maybe not.

Sympathetic and Gerry didn't really go together.

. . .

I swiped a clod of dirt off my forehead before digging a shovel back into the mound to my left. For the zillionth time that evening, I hefted a shovelful of earth from the pile and dumped it into the nearly full grave.

I swear, Sam and Dean made it look so easy.

Sure, I could have used the backhoe, but it just didn't feel right. Not after Gerry's warning. If someone were hunting me, wouldn't I have heard about it?

Where? In your freaking knitting circle?

My bitchy self had a point. I didn't talk to anyone except for Gerry. Where else was I going to learn this shit?

Digging my shovel back into the dwindling mound of dirt, I sighed. It had only been a year, but I was already tired of this shit. Tired of never running out of bad people to drink down. Tired of all the horrible things I saw when I read their blood.

Tired of not having a home, of jumping from one abandoned squatter's nest after the other.

I didn't know why I tried to stay near here. There was nothing left of my childhood home. I'd gone back, even though I'd known I shouldn't. All that had been there was a burned-out shell of a house and not much else.

And the graves of my parents? Those had been real.

My gaze lifted from the fresh mound of dirt to the

direction my parents were buried. I'd been the only one who'd woken up that night. I'd been the only one to turn into whatever the hell I was. My best guess? I was some kind of vampire. Even though the ones I'd met— okay, *ate*—didn't look too much like me.

For starters, my fangs were nothing like theirs. No needles for teeth or anything like that. No, when my fangs grew, they just looked like longer, sharper canines. And my eyes never got that eerie red glow, either. Instead, they were more of a vibrant purple. I drank blood—and a lot of it—and I was for sure nocturnal, but otherwise? I felt pretty normal.

Mostly. If by normal you meant a vengeful, supernatural creature with a soul-eating habit, then sure. Normal was my middle name.

I tamped my shovel down on the dirt, smacking the fluffy earth into a hard-packed mound before sprinkling a heavy dose of grass seed. Next was the water. After that, I gathered my supplies, rolled up the hose, and put everything back where it belonged, flipping off the backhoe like it had done me wrong.

Honestly, Gerry was lucky I hadn't shoved those keys up his ass.

Dirty, sweaty, and more irritated than anyone as deadly as I was had a right to be, I climbed back into my pilfered ride and started the engine. The man I'd stolen it from wasn't going to be using it anytime soon.

Or ever, really.

I'd enjoy one last cruise in it before donating it to the local wrecking yard. A shame since it was the nicest vehicle I'd ever semi-owned.

I wanted to think this would be the last time I'd be digging a grave. I wanted to think this would be the last time I'd have to. But I was lying to myself, the same way I'd lied to myself a year ago when I thought the police could have helped me, or that this life was all one big joke.

Denial was a real bitch sometimes.

3

The wind bit into my flesh as I perched on the ledge of an abandoned building the next night. If I had any sense, I would be in a lounge chair sipping a warm drink as I did my nightly surveillance, but apparently, I was a masochist. At nearly four in the morning, it was a little too close to dawn for my liking, and the wind was keeping me awake.

The sun wouldn't burn me, but I would be lethargic in the daylight. Plus, the closer it got to dawn, the closer I was to my internal night-night time. It wasn't like I'd drop dead or anything, but I wouldn't be a picnic to deal with, either. Plus, the closer to daylight it was, the harder I'd find it to do what I was on the godforsaken ledge for in the first damn place.

The building I was spying on had to be an arcane

club of some kind. It wasn't like members of the arcane wore a sign or anything, but it didn't take a genius to pick them out of a crowd. Their skin was just a little too pretty, their eyes just a little too jaded, their posture just a little off. They moved with a fluid sort of poise that no human could emulate. Like they were in charge of every millimeter of their bodies.

I said "their," but I fell under the arcane world, too, now didn't I? Which was a fact that I was not at all comfortable with. Every single member of the arcane I'd met had been a sleazeball of the highest order. I wasn't too keen on lumping myself in that group if I could help it.

I watched this club with a fair bit of regularity. I didn't trust members of the arcane world. In my experience—and based on what I'd gleaned from the secrets hidden in their blood—sooner or later, humans always paid the price for their existence. They were their victims, their food, or at times, their playthings.

I couldn't count how many attacks I'd stopped in the last year. Couldn't count how many people I'd stopped from dying. Sure, I wasn't picky about my meals—human, arcane, whatever—but the second I caught an arcaner doing something they shouldn't, I took them out. If I could stop just one girl waking up like I did, well, I was doing something right.

I could feel the bass notes through my feet a building away as the club rocked on into the night. Last call had to be sometime soon, right? Checking my watch, I sighed. Three fifty-five. Last call would be in three... two... one...

The ding of the last-call bell clanged so hard I could hear it over the din of the club. If I were a human, I wouldn't be able to hear the dance music through the heavily insulated walls, but with my freaky ears, I could. I couldn't imagine being on the inside of the building. My head would likely explode from the sheer noise alone.

Shivering, I yanked a cropped strand of hair out of my face and vainly tried to tuck it behind my ear. On top of the thirst for blood, weird purple eyes, and new nocturnal schedule, the ghostly white hair was another tick in the "weird" column. Honestly, I might as well tattoo "freak" on my forehead and call it a day. If I was going to perch on the ledge of a building like some macabre gargoyle, I should probably be smart enough to at least don a beanie and a sweatshirt. The leather pants were cute and all, but they didn't cover all of me.

I was too busy lamenting the loss of my brunette hair and green eyes—and my solidly packed wardrobe filled with decent winter clothes—that I missed it when the door opened the first time. Club-goers streamed in groups toward the full parking lot, all except a dark-haired woman. Instead of the well-lit lot, she turned down a particularly dark alley. She hunched in on herself like she was fighting the cold, her steps not as smooth as the typical arcaner.

Was she human?

Humans occasionally frequented clubs like this one, but often, they had an escort or were in a padded illusion of safety that only a group could provide. This girl was alone, walking down an alley just like I had before Jacob found me.

I knew, logically, that Jacob hadn't made me like this —that he hadn't been the one to turn me into a monster —but I still blamed him all the same.

Groaning, I stood to get a better vantage on the girl. If I didn't move, I'd lose her, and something in the back of my mind told me to follow. Told me to make sure she stayed safe. That teensy niggle of unease turned into a screeching alarm when I spied a tall man slam out of the club. His head covered in a dark hood, I couldn't quite make out the features of his face, save for the faint luminescence coming from the general vicinity of his eyes.

He tilted his head back, seeming to sniff the air before he whipped it in the direction of the woman.

Shit.

Without much consideration on my part, I promptly

hauled my ass to the fire escape. I'd totally tried that whole "jump off a building" thing a year ago, and there would never be any superhero landings for me. Not anymore.

Jumping off a building hurt. A lot.

I slid down the ladder like this was not my first rodeo —maybe my fourth or fifth—managing to avoid landing on a noisy aluminum trashcan. Barely. I could not, however, avoid the crunch of my thick boots landing on a glass bottle. I supposed I was just fortunate that the damn thing didn't defy the laws of physics and slip out from under my boot like a banana peel. Luckily, my prey was a little too preoccupied with his quarry to pay any attention to me or the seemingly deafening crunch of glass.

A calming breath was in order, but I just couldn't spare the time. I'd lost sight of both the girl and the guy, and as awesome as my sense of smell was, it wasn't like I was part bloodhound. I couldn't just sniff the air like the man had. Out-in-the-open scents dissipated faster than I could smell them. Still, I had a good idea where the guy was headed, so as quietly as I could, I advanced in that direction, praying the shush of my boots didn't make that much of a racket.

The alley smelled of urine, old trash, human waste, new trash, and ozone. Being so close to an arcane club, the ozone smell wasn't exactly surprising. I hadn't seen a lot of it—not outside of my prey trying to get away—but magic had a scent all on its lonesome, and spent magic had a very distinct smell.

The faint strains of a woman's distress reached me as they echoed off the nearby buildings, her fear and pain hitting me square in the gut. Done with worrying about the noise, I sprinted toward my quarry. My fangs had already begun to descend, their sharp points ready and willing to tear into the man's throat.

I hadn't been hungry a second ago, but the thought of ripping his throat open, the thought of making him cry out instead of her, made me fucking ravenous.

It didn't take too long to catch up to them. The woman was on the ground, scrambling backward in a pitiful little crab walk away from the man as the filth of the alleyway stained her jeans. The thud of the man's boots ricocheted through my chest as he stepped closer to her. Magic bloomed over his hands, and based on that alone, I was fairly certain he was a mage of some kind.

Mages were tricky, crafty little buggers. I hadn't come across too many, the majority of them preferring to do their dirt away from prying eyes. If I let him get a hit in, I would be hurting, so my best—hell, my only—course of action was to knock his ass out before he caught on that I was there.

All of this would have been easy to do if the woman hadn't alerted him to my presence right as I was about to strike. Honestly. Was the deep Scarlet Ohara gasp really necessary?

The man spun, his trajectory now target-locked on me. Unerringly, his magic hit me square in the chest, knocking me into a brick wall, hard enough that I heard it crumble beneath me.

I could tell the spell he'd used was probably meant for someone with a little less power than I possessed, because while hitting the wall stung a bit, it didn't actually hurt—no matter what my back, knees, hips, and skull said.

They were lying bastards, anyway.

Peeling myself out of the Sloane-sized dent in the bricks, I steeled myself for another blow.

But instead of hitting me again, he tried warning me off. "This is none of your business. Back off."

I couldn't see his face any better from this angle than I could at the top of the building. Damn mage tricks. He'd probably spelled his hood so it hid his face.

"Or what? You'll wave your sparkle fingers at me again?" I couldn't stop the taunting chuckle that slipped past my lips. "Nah, I think I'd rather have a snack."

He took a step back, seeming to expect me to lunge again, which revealed who he regularly dealt with.

Dumb fighters struck when the opponent could see them. Smart ones did not. No, I zigged when he expected me to zag, coming at him from the side with a solid kick to his knee. I felt more than heard the pop as his knee gave way when I brought my fist down on his temple. Sparkle Fingers managed to move at the last second, so my blow only glanced off the side of his head rather than landing square. Unfortunately for him, he was introduced to the business end of my knee, the sickening crunch of his nose breaking both gross and supremely satisfying. The sight of his eyes rolling back in his head more so.

Blood drip, drip, dripped, and I felt each individual drop as they hit the ground. My hunger slammed into me, but there was no way I could drink this guy down in front of a witness.

As divine as his blood smelled, I was hungry, *not* stupid.

Still, it took a few moments too long for my attention to break from the blood and land on the woman. Shaking myself, I managed to get my bloodlust under control.

"You okay?" I called to the shivering woman. She should be, she was sitting smack-dab in the middle of a puddle. "Did he hurt you?"

She shook her head, her movement a little too

manic, a little too wobbly, her long braids half-hiding her face. "N-no. Yo-you st-stopped him. Th-thank you."

I suddenly wished I had something warm to offer her, but all I had was what I was wearing. She probably had a home. I did not. The guy, though, had on a warm jacket. Reaching down, I yanked the fabric off his shoulders, tugging the sleeves free with only a few rips to show for it.

"Here." I offered her the pilfered coat. "You'll freeze."

Still shaking, she just stared up at me. "Wh-why did you help me? Most people would have ju-just walked on by."

Could I explain a year's worth of drama in a single pithy quote?

No, I could not.

The best I could do was give her a shrug. "I'm just not built that way." I offered her a hand up. "Get warm, get home, and for fuck's sake, stay out of alleys. They aren't safe."

Holding out the coat, I impatiently waited for her to slide into it. She blinked at me, belatedly catching the hint and slipped her arms into the sleeves. There, good deed done, and all that. It was dinnertime.

"Off you go. Lighted paths and no alleys, got it?" I

advised, turning my head to the blissfully tangy aroma of the mage's blood.

"I really do feel sorry about this," she muttered, and I whipped my head back to her a fraction too late.

Arms banded around my shoulders from behind, as the woman I'd just saved blew a handful of white dust in my face. The powder hit me like a stack of bricks as I lost control over my limbs. Unconsciousness didn't hit me right away, so I saw the regret filling her expression a split second before I was pulled into darkness.

After waking up at the foot of your own grave, anytime you woke up in a place you didn't remember bedding down in was a bit of a shock. Hence why I popped up off the cement floor like a fucking jack-in-the-box, ready to fight whoever or whatever was closest. It would figure that instead of being in the middle of a war, I was smack-dab in the middle of a cell.

It was a nice one, as far as cells went, but it was a cell, nonetheless. A concrete floor was beset on three sides by gray cinderblock walls, their faces carved with symbols I couldn't decipher. The back of the gray room held a made-up cot with a plush mattress, pillows, and a duvet. Beside it was a privacy screen, with tiny pink flowers hand-painted on the rice paper panels that hid what I hoped was a toilet. In front of the privacy screen was a small table with a stool nestled underneath, topped with a few books, a tray of food, and a pad of sketch paper.

No pens or pencils were in sight, instead there was a familiar wooden box next to the pad. I knew if I opened it, my favorite brand of charcoals would be inside. I couldn't say why, but just looking at that box made me want to smash it. My mother had bought me a set—grudgingly, I might add—when I was eight. My art teacher, Mr. Sigmund, had reverently showed us his set, and the Japanese brand did not come cheap. I'd begged six months for that set, and when my mother routinely told me no, I saved my allowance for it. I mowed lawns for it, raked leaves, pulled weeds. But the set of charcoals were expensive, and regardless of my little eight-year-old drive, I wouldn't be able to afford them.

She'd surprised me with that very set for my birthday, and I'd burst into tears, hugging her so tight. I remembered how her hair smelled that day, like jasmine and citrus, and the first thing I'd drawn with my brand-new charcoals had been my mother's face. I was eight, and it was in no way a masterpiece, but my mom kept that picture in her pocketbook.

A pocketbook that was likely burned to ash just like everything else we ever had. Just like my parents.

"Do you like them?" a woman asked, and I slowly turned my gaze to the fourth wall. It wasn't a wall at all but a cell door, the bars etched with the same symbols as the walls. Likely the markings were spells meant to keep me in. Keep me trapped.

The woman was sitting on a plain metal folding chair, one leg crossed over the other, her air of confidence ill-fitting her choice of seat. She wore a pristine white pants suit, a black crew-neck top, with a pair of zebra-print stilettos on her feet. I couldn't tell if they were real or a knockoff, but if the red soles and crisp lines of the suit were any indication, then they were likely as real as they got. Her hair was a wavy auburn that was just a shade lighter than true red, with a pair of eyes an odd reddish-whiskey color that reminded me of fresh-spilled blood but could pass for brown to a less-discerning eye.

She wasn't old nor was she young. Really, she appeared my mother's age, the faint kiss of time fanning out from her eyes. She had a tiny little upturn to her nose, which should make her appear cute, but I had a feeling this lady hadn't been called cute *ever*, and she'd probably gut the first dumb bastard to try.

"The charcoals," she prompted like I was simple, "do you like them?"

I flashed my teeth in a failed attempt at a smile. "To be honest?" She nodded for me to continue. "I'm having a hell of a time not smashing them to slivers."

She gave me a smile in return, only hers was genuine and not a bearing of teeth and fangs. "Your candor is refreshing, Sloane. As are your actions." She uncrossed her legs and recrossed them, her left switching places with the right. She settled onto her chair, too, resting her back on the unyielding metal. "When we picked you up, I was under the impression we'd be putting down a mass-murdering Rogue, not a perky blonde with a do-gooder attitude."

Her words didn't smell like the truth—and I couldn't tell you *how* I knew she was bullshitting me, I just did. Still, I had no intention for the word to slip from my mouth, even though it did without consulting my brain.

"Liar."

The woman's smile widened like she was pleased. Then, she sighed like I was giving her a present, the sheer relish on her face enough to turn my stomach. "Oh, I'm going to like you, Sloane."

I couldn't say why, but that statement was not comforting. Not at all.

"My name is Emrys Zane, and I run the Night

Watch." At my blinking confusion, she elaborated, gesturing at my cell. "This is the Night Watch. Well, a part of it. Typically, we don't hold many people down here. The ABI carts off the ones they see fit for trial. Very few even see these cells. The Night Watch takes the cases the ABI refuse to, or rather, too scared to take."

"ABI?" I asked, unfamiliar with the acronym.

"Arcane Bureau of Investigation, the arcane world's police. If the ABI are the police, the Night Watch would be the bounty hunters. There are several branches of the ABI, but only one of the Night Watch."

While all this was *super* fascinating, I had a feeling she wasn't holding me here for tea and cookies. That girl in the alley had been a setup. They'd known I couldn't stop myself from helping someone in trouble. They'd *known* I would show up. The question was: why? But I didn't ask, content on letting Emrys carry on with her pitch.

"Do you know about the bounty on your head, Sloane? What it's up to?"

Considering I had no idea I even had a bounty out for me, the answer was a resounding "no."

"Can't say I do. I hope it's big." I wasn't being very nice, but I had the distinct feeling that Emrys wouldn't appreciate subterfuge.

"Three million," she murmured, the quiet words landing like a blow.

"Dollars?" I blurted, shocked anyone would be that desperate to have my head. Then again... I had killed a lot of people over the last year. A lot.

Emrys gave me a grave sort of nod. "Rather remarkable, really. There hasn't been a bounty that high in ages. You know the funny part?"

I shrugged, tossing my hands up, exasperated. "I'm sure you're going to tell me."

Emrys chuckled, before delivering another blow. "The bounty was coded for alive only and would be forfeit upon your death. I find that very interesting, Sloane. Don't you?"

I couldn't for the life of me understand why someone would want me captured alive. Maybe to study me? Torture me? Kill me themselves? None of that spelled happy things.

"Interesting is not the word I would use." I plopped down on the edge of the mattress. "You lied before, why? Did you think I wouldn't smell it, or was it a test?"

"Everything is always a test, dear. Life is a test," she said cryptically. "Yes, I wanted to know if you could sense a lie, but more, I wanted to know if you'd call me on it. You've killed over two hundred members of the arcane, not to mention an unknown number of humans. I wanted to know who I was dealing with."

If she set up the trap, she knew exactly what kind of person I was. And she was wrong. I'd killed over three hundred members of the arcane and roughly a hundred humans. "Liar."

Surprise crossed her face at that one. "No, I did not lie," she insisted, affront clear in her tone. "I have record of only two hundred and six members of the arcane missing, presumed dead, at your hand."

Now, I could confess and let her do whatever she was going to do, but letting her stew in her own misinformation sounded much more fun.

"Your records are wrong." I yawned before falling back on the rather soft mattress. It had been a while since I'd had a good bed to sleep in. Abandoned buildings and comfy home furnishings didn't exactly go hand in hand. Toeing off my boots, I got comfortable, allowing my body to sink into the plush softness. "What I'd really love to know is how many were on your books before I *allegedly* picked them off like the leeches they were? How many I caught doing things they shouldn't? How many with souls as black as night and twice as foul?"

Emrys narrowed her eyes at me, uncrossing her legs so both spindly heels were on the ground. She could be pissed all she wanted to, I was going to enjoy the pillow and blanket. Snuggling into the bed, I closed my eyes. If I was stuck here, I might as well enjoy it. I had a feeling I wouldn't exactly be skipping once she delivered me to whoever posted that ridiculous bounty.

"And how would you know how dark their souls were?"

I cracked an eyelid, shooting her an "oh, please" look. "You know my favorite brand of charcoals, but you don't know this?" I snorted and turned to my side to really enjoy the mattress. "The sins of every man, woman, and arcaner are hidden in the blood, sweetheart."

I closed my cracked lid, but both my eyes popped open at the screech of the chair skidding. Emrys was on her feet, a mere inch from the bars. I, however, was still in bed, staring at the formerly collected woman, her reddish eyes glowing at me.

"You read their blood, correct? Their souls. And that's why you killed them all. Because they were evil." She may have started it as a question, but Emrys seemed to be working the details out on her own. "A soul reader," she whispered under her breath, the title filled with a reverence I didn't understand.

Maybe I didn't want to understand.

With that, she abruptly turned and strode out of sight, a loud clanging of a metal door sealing shut punctuating her departure. And as much as I would have loved to settle into the plush mattress, I was instead filled with the distinct impression that I should have kept my mouth shut.

My internal clock was reading that dawn was approaching again when the tell-tale squeak of hinges signaled someone's arrival. The meal left for me was cold and congealed and one hundred percent undisturbed.

I had no desire to be drugged, thank you.

But that also meant I was a might bit peckish, AKA, hungry enough to eat a bear.

Unlike the delicate tap of Emrys' shoes, the heavy steps coming my way signaled a *hugely* different visitor. I propped myself up on my pillows, wanting to see the man who was likely here to lead me to my doom. He was dark-haired and tan-skinned, a wealth of stubble on his cheeks and chin, like using a razor was a personal affront. He wore a black shirt, leather pants, and boots, and held himself delicate like he was hurt as he lowered himself onto the chair. Instead of looking at me, he raked a hand through his hair and sighed.

His exhaustion was real enough, but I knew—*don't ask me how*—this was an act. He smelled of half-truths and deception. Unlike Emrys, I decided not to call him on it. A faint scent tickled the air, faint, barely there, but I smelled it all the same. It was a familiar scent, and my fangs descended all on their very lonesome.

But it wasn't just because I was hungry. It was because I knew exactly who he was.

His pale-hazel gaze met my purple one.

The guy from the alley.

5

Sparkle Fingers—as he would be dubbed until I actually knew his name—was a ball of giggles. He exuded happiness and light and exactly zero hostility or malice.

Deep grooves wrinkled the space between his eyes as he regarded me like one would a clump of dog shit on their boot. Honestly? It was like I was staring at my own personal executioner. A personal executioner with a now-crooked nose that seemed to still need some mending.

A very crazy part of me wanted to giggle at him just to see if his head would explode. I mean, what was I going to do? Run away screaming?

I was stuck in this cell with nowhere to run and no place to hide. I hadn't messed with the runes carved in the walls or bars—my gleaned-yet-limited knowledge had warned me not to try. At least the sins I read in the blood I drank was good for something, other than the inevitable spiral into mental illness. Information was always a good thing to have.

Plus, he seemed cranky, and I had no place else to be. Might as well make this shit fun.

"Come to take me away already? Shame. I was just getting cozy." I punctuated my words by wiggling in the mussed covers, showing him just *how* cozy I found them.

Sparkle's frown deepened as he scratched his fingers through the stubble on his cheek. He sniffed and then winced, his hand moving to cover his nose before he thought better of it. "You seem pretty happy with your accommodations. I've never seen someone so pleased to have a bed."

His voice sounded different than when he'd warned me off in the alley, his accent losing its American and landing solidly in British territory. *Faker.*

"How's the nose? Have you had it reset yet?" He opened his mouth to likely bullshit me, but I stopped him. "And before you feign surprise, I know it was you in that alley. You still have blood on you, Cupcake, and you smell delicious." I let my otherness peek out of my eyes as I showed him a bit of fang.

I figured he would startle—it was what every other

arcaner had done when they saw my teeth—but his frown only deepened.

"Look, I don't want you here. None of us want you here. But Emrys seems to think you're worth saving, and I'd rather follow her orders than anyone else's. She's willing to say you went rabid and had to be put down." He stopped, shaking his head before shooting to his feet. "She's willing to void a three-million-dollar contract."

Man, this guy was excitable. Sparky started pacing the corridor in front of my cell, and every time he tried breathing through his nose, he would just get more and more pissed off.

"I take it this favor comes at a price?" I called on his third pass because old Sparky wasn't talking, and I was getting bored with the sales pitch.

He stomped back to my cell door, hissing when his skin made contact with the bars. I could hear his flesh sizzling. I could smell it, too. Not. Appetizing.

"If you think we're just going to void a three-million-dollar contract out of the goodness of our hearts..." He pushed off the bars, his macho show of strength over.

"But it's not 'we,' is it? You aren't doing shit. She's voiding the contract. What I want to know is what's expected out of me? Nothing's free in this world, Sparky, I know that. So, what does she want?"

There were things I couldn't do. *Wouldn't* do. As

mercenary a bitch as I was, I wouldn't kill people who didn't deserve it. I wouldn't hurt children, *ever*. And I wasn't going to be anyone's slave. If any of those rules were going to be violated, she might as well truss me up, hand me over, and get her payday.

Because the other option would *not* go well for her.

I told Sparky as much.

"I don't think you understand the gravity of your situation," he began, his condescending tone raking against my nerves.

My chuckle was dark and forbidding. "I think it's you who doesn't understand. I have nothing to lose. Not one thing you could hold against me. I don't have a home or a family or a life. I cannot be bought or bribed or bargained with. She wants to void the contract, fine. That's her choice. What I'm willing to do in return is mine. Now"—Prompted, I got up from my very cozy, very missed bed—"why don't you quit your bullshit posturing, and tell me what she wants in return."

Sparky huffed, slamming himself back onto the chair like a petulant child. I waited, slipping on my boots as he debated with himself on whether or not he was going to sack up and answer me.

"Emrys thinks you're valuable." He spat the words like an accusation. "She wants to recruit you." He let loose a spectacular sneer. "Why she would want a murderer on the team is beyond me. But I follow orders, as will you."

Awww, he doesn't want me in his sandbox. Poor baby.

I couldn't say it, but I agreed with him. I *was* a murderer. If I looked at myself with any rational thought, I *was* the bad guy.

And maybe? They were safer with me in this cage than they would be with me out of it.

Still, giving him shit was much more fun than wallowing. "I kill people who deserve it, and in exchange, I get a little dinner. Would you look so callously at a lion, Sparky?"

His face turned an unhealthy shade of crimson before the door squeaked again. Light, barely-there footsteps were followed by an irritated female voice.

"You were supposed to bring her upstairs, not yak her ear off," the dainty girl with the dark braids and a smokey voice said, her small frame dwarfed by Sparky, even though he was sitting down. In the light, I recognized her as the girl from the alley, her golden skin no longer blueish with the cold. The girl dismissed him, giving him her back as she turned to me. "I'm sorry about him. He's just mad you broke his nose. I'm Dahlia, by the way."

She gave me a weird sort of wave, and then I realized she was doing intricate hand movements of a spell. The runes in my cell began to glow white, the heat of them almost scalding before the markings dimmed. The sound of a key turning in a lock rang through the room, even though it appeared as if she had no key. Then, she gripped the bars that had scalded Sparky's fingers just moments ago and swung the door wide.

Her expression was sheepish when I hesitated to leave the cell. "I really am sorry about drugging you. We thought... Well, we were under the impression you were..."

"A ravenous monster with no control and no scruples?" I quipped. "Yeah, I caught that."

Her wince only grew. "But you saved me. I know I didn't really need saving, but you thought I did. You even gave me a coat when I was cold. Monsters don't do that."

Her mind seemed to be made up—she nodded and stepped away from the door so I could exit. But it wasn't Dahlia I was worried about. Sparky was still sitting in the chair, mulishly staring at me like I was going to rip out her throat at any second. *Idiot.*

Rather than give him the satisfaction of seeing me weak, I strode through the door, giving him my back as soon as I was out. And then he did exactly what I knew he would, the prick.

He pounced.

I could feel the movement before it ever reached me, the rough push of air as he lunged. In this tight of a space, I could feel every breath he took, smell the scent of his rage hit its peak, and this close? I could hear his heart pick up speed at the very last second as his adrenaline kicked in.

So, when he tried to grab me, he clutched nothing but air.

But I wasn't as foolish. In his daze, I latched onto his shirt and slammed him into the gray wall hard enough that the stone hissed with a crack before depositing him ass over tea kettle on the floor. I grabbed his face, smooshing his cheeks and mouth with my fingers, waiting for his eyes to finally focus. When they did, I wanted to make sure he understood. I wouldn't be keeping one eye open. I wouldn't be watching my back. I was the apex predator in this scenario, not him.

And I would not be fucked with.

"The only reason you aren't dead already, is because I was trying to spare your victim from seeing me spill your blood all over the street. Attack me again, and I won't give a shit if the Pope sees, I'll gut you like a fucking fish and lick my fingers clean afterward. Don't test me, Sparky. I don't make the same mistake twice." Then, I may have bounced his stupid head off the floor as I skipped to follow Dahlia.

Okay, the skipping was probably a little petty, but whatever.

The rest of the holding area appeared similar to my cell, but there weren't many, maybe five other small rooms like mine. Only, none of them were furnished. No cot, no toilet, no desk, or screen. Each room was just cinderblock walls filled with the same runes that were in my cell. So, either they didn't get many visitors, or...

"I know how it looks." Dahlia's voice broke me from my musings. "But we don't have very many people as guests in that part of the house. Usually we make the hand off to the ABI. No muss, no fuss. I can't think of a time when there was actually a visitor in those cells."

"So, the house came equipped with a dungeon?"

She swept a handful of braids off her shoulder as she shrugged. "I'm not sure. I think it might have been a lycanthropes moon-called area at one time, but I don't really know the specifics."

My feet stuttered to a stop. "Lycanthropes?"

Dahlia took a few more steps before she noticed I wasn't following. "Wow, you're new. Yes, lycanthropes are a thing. Totally different from weres and shifters, by the way. Lycanthropes are humans infected with a specific type of rabies that mutates their DNA. It makes them turn into these weird half-man, half-animal creatures on the full moon that are *not* cute. Those went pretty much extinct a few decades ago after the ABI cracked down on the mad scientist sorcerer who was trying to 'make' weres."

At my wide eyes due to the veritable fount of information, she waved her hand at me like she was erasing her words from the air. It didn't matter. I'd seen more than a few on my one-woman rampage of Ascension.

Could a year-long culling be called a rampage?

"Don't even ask. Anyway, where was I?" She seemed to think on it for a second. "Right. Weres are arcaners with the ability to shift into a specific animal, and shifters—or shapeshifters—can change into any animal within reason. Both species have their mind intact, but are slightly more animalistic. Except for the lycanthropes. Those guys are coo-coo."

When she was done exploding my brain with info, she gestured for me to get moving, which I did, but with a definite wariness in my step.

"Emrys wants me to show you around the house before your meeting. Plus, the longer we give Bastian to calm down after getting his ass kicked for the second time in twenty-four hours, the better. Man, I've never seen him so cranky."

So Sparky was named Bastian. Short for Sebastian, I was guessing. I liked Sparky better.

"I think he's just mad he doesn't get the payday," I

muttered, but I knew that wasn't true. I'd likely bruised his fragile male ego, and as much as I didn't want to, I was going to have to watch my back.

Dahlia snorted, the indelicate sound endearing on the small woman. And she was tiny. I was maybe five eight. She had to be barely pushing five foot even, and that was a stretch. But it wasn't just that she was short, it was how thin she was. I wouldn't have put her past eighteen years old, but I knew she had to be older. She had that look arcaners got when they'd seen some shit.

"Maybe," she mused. "But I think he's more afraid of you. He's one of the strongest of us—outside of Emrys and Thomas. I think he sees you as a danger for the people he cares about."

Shit. Now I felt slightly bad about spiking his head on the ground like a volleyball.

Maybe more than slightly.

6

I didn't say anything else as Dahlia continued leading me up a set of stairs to a thick metal door. At the door, she made a set of complicated hand motions, and the sound of a key in a lock rang out again like when she opened my cell.

With a faint hiss, the door cracked, and she yanked on the metal with all her strength before opening it wide to reveal a sort of opulence I was ill-prepared for. The floors were a dark wood with whorls of grain intricately swirling in each plank, the whole of which practically gleamed against the light of the delicate sconces and lamps dotting around what I assumed was a great room.

A wide staircase lay to my left, the newel post thick and forbidding and topped with a falcon with its wings spread wide. There were bookcases tucked in nooks and crannies, soft furniture that appeared far too expensive for me to sit on, and more that I couldn't see but knew was there just based on this one room.

But really?

It was the architecture that really got me. It was the high vaulted ceilings and wide windows, the hand-carved moldings and detail. Whoever had built this place had loved it—loved it more than rest or sleep—because it must have taken years to craft all of this.

I should have figured a house with a damn dungeon would be huge, but I still managed to be caught unaware. Somehow, I seemed to feel safer in the dungeon than if I stepped out into the house proper—even with Sparky's boots clomping like a herd of buffalo behind me.

Those stomping feet—and maybe the rage laced in every stomp—were what propelled me out of the dungeon and into the great room. Dahlia hadn't stopped, she was heading up the stairs and I had to run to catch up. And if I managed to slam the heavy dungeon door in Sparky's face, well, it was totally unintentional and not at all on purpose.

My feet practically sank into the plush carpet on the stairs, the delicate pattern swirling up the steps like a wave. Maybe it was the artist in me, but I loved a well-put-together design, and everything about this place had the feel of care, of time. It made me wistful of my parent's house. That wistfulness quickly turned bitter in my chest, and I had to swallow down the hurt and rage and...

Before we reached the top landing, a head poked over the rail. Slitted green eyes and a scowling face stared right at me, rage tinting her features. Her face was positively elfin, despite the septum piercing and heavy eye makeup.

"Stop it. If you're coming up here, you need to ward your mind. It's one thing for me to deal with that bullshit outside," the small woman griped at me, her body coming into full view as we crested the landing. She gestured to the windows, waving at them like she was warding off the outside world. "But if you think I'm carrying your emotions while I'm inside my own damn home, you've got another thing coming. If you're going to be in this house, you need to figure your shit out."

Slightly startled that such a tiny person could be filled with so much rage, I cast a wide-eyed glance to Dahlia.

"Crap. I knew I forgot something," Dahlia groaned. "Don't worry, Harper. I'll get her warded in a few." She then turned back to me. "Harper, this is Sloane, our new recruit."

Harper growled, not sparing me another glance. "I

don't give a fuck who she is. Ward her and then tell her to stay out of my rooms. Got it?"

I couldn't help it, I snorted. Harper and I were going to be besties. I just knew it.

"Wow." That was something else. I needed to figure out who pissed in her Cheerios and hand them a medal or something. Their irritation game had to be top notch.

Dahlia sighed before turning back to me. "Harper is an empath. One of the stronger ones. If you're within a mile of her, she can feel your emotions, which doesn't help with the whole sanity bit. I'll let Emrys ward you. Hers are the best."

"Ward me?"

She nodded, chewing on a fingernail. "Emrys is a druid. One of the last in the Americas. Not too many immigrated here, or the ones who did, didn't make it too long on this continent. South America has quite a few more, and Canada has a handful, but she's one of the last of her kind. She can ward you so tight, Harper won't have a reason to bitch at you. Which is good, because if she hates you, it's unlikely that she'll share the Wi-Fi password. Or program your tech. Or do just about anything else that requires any lick of technology. She's our tech wizard."

Dahlia paused, before wiping the air like she was erasing something. "She's not actually a wizard, by the way. She's just awesome at it. She runs comms on jobs and keeps us out of all CCTV footage. But also? The computers interfere with the whole emotions thing. If she could feel you from her room, you must have been feeling some heavy shit. She'll likely be a complete bitch to you until you get that fixed."

"Get warded pronto. Check." I gave Dahlia a thumbs-up, letting her know I for sure got it.

"Follow me. I'll introduce you to Simon before you meet with Emrys and Thomas."

We turned right down the corridor toward a closed door decorated with "Keep Out" and "No Girls Allowed" signs. Granted, the "No Girls Allowed" sign had a piece of paper attached to it with Scotch tape with the words "Dahlia is okay" hastily written on it, the frayed edge of the paper jagged like it had been ripped out of a spiral notebook. Dahlia pounded on the door with her fist.

We heard a "come in" before she opened the door. The inside of the room was just as messy as I figured it would be. A slender guy decked out in a beanie, glasses, and flannel shirt was sitting on a couch that had seen better days. In his hand was a gaming controller and he was playing some kind of game that required a cat to fight element-wielding foes.

Not what I would expect out of a grown man, but

who was I to judge his gaming needs? As long as he wasn't playing some shooter game, I was all for it.

"Simon, pause your silly cat game and meet Sloane."

Simon did not, in fact, pause his game. Instead he ignored my presence altogether while talking to Dahlia like I wasn't there. "She the one who has Harper in a twist?"

His accent was American with a faint British flair, not what I would have expected out of the mouth of a guy who wore flannel like it was his job.

"Don't be rude, Simon."

He grunted back at her, his slight shoulders shrugging. "You know the drill, babe. I don't make the rules."

"They're your rules. Of course you make the rules."

Just then, I felt something at my ankles, a slight brushing, and I glanced down. What I saw might have made me jump out of my skin if I weren't afraid I'd hurt it. A delicate amalgamation of bones in what I could only hope was the shape of a cat, brushed against my legs again like it was marking me. It was creepy as fuck and cute as hell, and I had to fight the urge not to try and pick it up. Its bones were stark white, but its eyes—which were just orbs of green smoke—cast a glow over its whole body.

I had a feeling I was supposed to be scared, but I just... wasn't. Mom had never let me have a cat, and I'd always wanted one. She said she was allergic, but I think she just didn't like that cats walked all over everything.

"Boy or girl?" I asked, instead of doing what I really wanted, which was to scoop it up and try and pet it.

"She's a girl." He paused, his words a little ruffled. "You're not scared?"

Instead of answering that stupid question, I plopped on the floor, crossing my legs as I got a better look at the skeleton kitty. "Can I pet her? What's her name?"

"Isis, and yeah. You sure you're not afraid?"

Dahlia snorted. "Not everyone is going to scream blue bloody murder and run screaming out of the house, Simon. You know that was a one-time thing."

That sounded like a story I wanted to hear, but I was busy letting the bone kitty smell my hand before I ran my fingers over her spine. "Isis, sweetheart, you are a gorgeous kitty. Don't let anyone tell you any different. If they run screaming, chase them and make them cry, okay?"

Isis jumped onto my lap, and I rubbed under her chin as she started to purr. "That's right, you fearsome little beast."

"Okay, you got my vote." Simon paused his game. "Why does Bastian hate her again?"

I snorted, but it was Dahlia who answered for me,

"It's either because she broke his nose and kicked his ass, or because she's a mass murderer."

Ouch. Yeah, "mass murderer" was a title I didn't like, but the truth hurt sometimes, right? "Don't forget, I just spiked his head off the concrete and called him Sparky. That won't win me any favors. But at least you like me, don't you, Isis?"

Simon chuckled. "And you brought her in here? You had better take her to Emrys before Bastian finds out and loses the last little bit of his mind."

"That's okay, I'll just hold you and scare him off, won't I?" I said to the cat who was now making herself at home under my chin.

Simon bleated out a guffaw. "How did you know it was Bastian who ran screaming from the house?"

"Common sense? Harper doesn't seem like the kind of girl who would hang out. Dahlia is allowed in, and Emrys is too cool and collected to run screaming from anywhere. Plus, the thought of Bastian running away from a kitty is the best fucking thing I've heard in ages." I cuddled the cat closer, her fragile bones pressing into my bare forearm. "Wanna come with me, Isis? I'll scratch your chin and behind where your ears should be. It'll be fun."

To Simon I said, "I want to steal your cat. She's adorable."

"Can't," Dahlia chimed in. "We're meeting with Thomas, too, and those two don't get along. Put the adorable kitty down. I'm sure Simon won't mind you playing with her later?"

I may or may not have pouted as I reluctantly set Isis on the floor, giving her extra chin rubs before I got up. "I guess, but if she goes missing? I totally took her and probably won't give her back. Cool?"

Simon shook his head. "I've met a few mass murderers in my day. Never met one who likes cats and talks to them like they're people before." He rolled his head on his neck to face Dahlia. "You're sure she's a killer? She seems so... nice."

I let my otherness leak out of my purple eyes, flashing a bit of fang as I answered his question. "I only kill bad people. If that helps you sleep at night, I mean."

Simon's eyes widened, and he shot Dahlia a look as he shoved himself up off the couch. "You'd better get her to Emrys. The last thing we need is Bastian seeing her like that in here. Scoot."

Simon practically shoved us out of the room as he scooped up Isis and held her to his chest. I gave her one last scratch before we were summarily ousted from Simon's room and the door closed and locked.

"Simon is Bastian's little brother," Dahlia informed me. "He's all the family Bastian has left."

Which made my heart hurt for reasons I didn't want to examine.

Harper's voice floated through a closed door to my left. "Get her warded, or so help me, I will pour water on the router and cut the hard line to the house!"

With the threat made against the Wi-Fi, Dahlia latched onto my arm, and the tiny woman dragged me down the hallway.

A meeting with Emrys.

Super.

7

Dahlia gestured for me to knock on the door before she backed away, like she was saving herself from the portal of my imminent doom. A few steps later, she spun and raced down the hallway back to Simon's room.

Without another option left—other than vaulting the banister and hauling ass out of the house—I knocked, just a gentle three-tap that was not all hesitant or weak sounding. Nope. I was completely and totally not nervous.

Less than a second later, the door flew open to reveal a tall man with jet-black hair and a wicked grin. The strands appeared soft to the touch as they swept the sides of his jaw, tickling the thick stubble there. His grin was a little too perfect, almost sinister, which was at odds with his blindingly white smile and full lips. Maybe it was his cheekbones that were just a little too sharp, or the odd green color of his eyes against his pale-bronze coloring. Or maybe it was because he was just a little too pretty, appeared a little too lethal.

Since he was not who I was expecting, I backed up a step, hoping Dahlia had gotten confused by the boatload of doors in the hall and mixed up where I was supposed to go. A hope that was dashed not a second later when the man's smile grew before he latched onto my arm with an iron grip and hauled me in the room. He let me go in the next instant, the momentum whirling me inside the office like a top.

I was strong—like "could bend metal with my bare hands" strong. This dude made me look and feel like a wimp, and even though he hadn't hurt me, I was one hundred percent certain he could have if he'd wanted to.

"Ah, good. I was wondering what was holding you up. Bastian decided to throw a fit, did he?" Emrys said from behind a stout desk, her eyes trained on a large monitor as she clicked her mouse. "I see you've met Thomas."

Thomas? Did she mean the man who could crush me to a pulp with a flick of his fingers? I turned to look at him, but he'd moved without me noticing. I scanned the room for him, only to find him sitting in a leather wingback with a glass of amber liquid in his right hand and a lit cigar in his left. His eyes had a faint glow to them that reminded me of mine when I got riled.

I had to say, Thomas did not give me the warm and fuzzies.

"Not formally, no," I muttered, feeling awkward and unsure of myself as I stood in the middle of Emrys' office like I was in to see the principal.

"My apologies. Where are my manners?" Thomas said from his perch before setting his cigar down in an ashtray. He stood faster than my gaze could track and then he was in my space, towering over me like a creeper.

Thomas was good looking and knew it. He also knew he was at the top of the food chain.

Message received.

"What manners?" I scoffed, pressing a hand to his chest and gently moving him out of my space. I knew without a doubt in my mind that he was moving of his own accord and wouldn't if he didn't want to be moved. It was tough not to roll my eyes. "I get it. You're stronger and faster and could crush me like a bug should the spirit move you."

"As long as we understand each other," Thomas drawled, catching my hand in his as he bowed his head to give it a light peck. "Thomas Gao, and you are Sloane Cabot."

I nodded before snatching my hand back.

"Quit antagonizing her, Thomas. That is not what you are here for, and you know it."

He sent Emrys a petulant glare before sauntering at a human's speed back to his chair. "If you must ruin my fun, fine."

"Take a seat, Sloane." Emrys gestured to the two leather club chairs across from her desk.

I chose the one farthest from Thomas, a fact he noted if his derisive snort was any indication.

"I called you up here—as I'm sure Sebastian informed you—to formally invite you to be a member of the Night Watch. On a probationary basis, of course. In exchange for your services for no less than one year, you will be provided a room, board, and a stipend for expenses. After your probationary period, you may move to be a full member of the Night Watch and awarded the clearance that provides."

"Whoa, whoa, whoa. I haven't said yes yet. I want to know what it is you do. Because delivering a girl to someone for three million dollars—and it not being the governing body that wants me, but a private citizen—doesn't make me too keen on being a member. It makes me think you're into some seriously shady shit. I might be a mass-murdering sociopath, lady, but I have scruples."

Emrys' lips tipped up like she thought I was cute. "We *didn't* deliver you anywhere. As far as the customer knows, you died and were incinerated by Bastian Cartwright himself after you attacked him. And to be fair, I only took the job, because if we hadn't, someone else would have. People with less *scruples*."

I crossed my arms and sat back in my chair. "You didn't answer my question. You're quite good at that. Not answering questions."

"It used to be my job once upon a time. Now, since you insist on knowing, you will read people for us using your abilities. Not bite, not kill. Just read."

I guessed she meant no soul-eating and no blood-drinking as well.

"That's going to be a problem," I muttered under my breath. "Couple of issues with that. I've never read anyone that I didn't bite first, for one. The 'reading,' as you call it, is involuntary on my part. Two, of the people I've bitten, I haven't left a single one alive. Three, I need to eat. Human food is fun and all, but I need blood to survive."

I may have left off that whole bit about the ones I killed, I also consumed their soul, but if she didn't know, I had no intention of informing her.

"Your maker should be dragged out on the street and shot. What in the bloody hell did they teach you?" Thomas griped, his words laced with venom.

"Maker?" I shook my head. "I woke up on the foot of my own grave a year ago. I don't have a maker, and I didn't choose this."

"All vampires have a maker." Thomas rolled his eyes at me like I was an idiot. "And you have to choose this life. The covenant prevents humans from being selected any other way." His voice was snide, like he was talking to a brainless little girl instead of the cold-blooded murderer I was.

I leaned forward in my seat and let my otherness emerge from my eyes. He wanted to think I was stupid? Fine. But I wasn't a liar.

"I don't, and I didn't." I could feel my fangs lengthening to their sharp points and digging into my bottom lip.

Before I knew it, Thomas was out of his seat and leaning over me. His fingers dug into the skin of my face as he studied my fangs and eyes. A light dawned on his expression before he let me go. "You're a blood drinker, but you're no vampire."

I knew I was different than other vampires—at least the bottom-feeding assholes I'd come across in the last year. I didn't have the red eyes or weird extra set of needle fangs that they all had.

"You, my dear, are what happens when two species mate that shouldn't."

Staring up at him, I wondered if I could punch him in the balls before he smashed my head in with his bare hands. "Excuse me?"

"If the ABI finds out about her, we're all dead. You know that, right?" Thomas griped at Emrys, before he put his glass to his lips and drank it down.

"I'm handling it. Why do you think you're here? As far as they are concerned, she is a newly minted vampire under your line, and what they don't know, will keep her and all of us alive."

Thomas scoffed. "I like my head attached to my shoulders, thank you very much. Why would I claim this little albatross?"

Emrys steepled her fingers as she rested her elbows on the arms of her chair. She leveled Thomas with an expression so piercing I had to turn away before she decided to look at me like that. "Because I already filed the paperwork, and you have no choice."

A few things made sense as I studied the room. As I stared at the bookcases lining the walls, I reordered the facts as I knew them. One: either my parents weren't human, or they weren't my real parents. Rosalind and Peter Cabot raised me. My first memory was a tea party my mother and I had with a special tea set that I'd gotten that Christmas. I was three. Two: If they weren't human, then I wasn't and never had been. Three: If I wasn't human, and neither were they, why was I here and they weren't? How was I alive?

Emrys and Thomas were still arguing, but they quit when my whispered question reached their ears. "What am I?"

Emrys, once again, answered my question without answering it at all. "You come from the union of a grave talker and a blood mage. Unlike grave talkers, you cannot see the dead, and unlike blood mages, you cannot wield blood magic. Your power is different, and because of the destruction you can cause, because of the secrets someone like you can glean, these two species are discouraged from breeding."

I shook my head, the equation just not adding up. "That doesn't make any sense. I was human. I ate cheeseburgers and argued with my mom about my major. I wasn't strong or fast and sure as shit didn't drink blood. No, someone did this to me. My parents were human. *I* was human."

Emrys' face was filled with pity. "Not if they bound you, dear. Which given the power your mother possessed, is highly likely. Rosalind Sawyer Cabot was a venerated blood mage. If your father was an unregistered grave talker, then they could have bound you and passed you off as a human uninherit. As a human, you could have easily gone to a vampire to turn you."

Thomas groaned and stomped over to a set of glass decanters filled with amber liquid. "What she is failing to say, is that by hiding you and lying to them, our heads will be on the chopping block if anyone finds out what you are."

I'd thought of little else besides what had happened to my parents, to my life, in the last year. The scenarios were many and far-reaching, one just as preposterous as the next. I didn't remember much past falling asleep one night and waking up in that damn cemetery. There wasn't a single clue in our burned-out home, not one scent, not a shred of anything to tell me what happened.

"Did they kill them?" Was that my voice that sounded like broken glass? Were those tears racing down my cheeks?

Thomas scoffed at me, my idiocy too much for him to bear. "You think you'd have been left alive if the ABI had that first inkling you existed? No, Sloane. Whatever happened to your parents? It wasn't the ABI."

My hand swiped at my face, dashing the tears off my cheeks as I sucked in a breath to calm my racing heart.

"That still doesn't solve our most basic problem." I held up a hand to stop Thomas from interjecting more of his shitty commentary. "Besides staying hidden and not bringing down the wrath of the evil government agency upon us, I know. I have to eat. Vampire or not, I'm a blood drinker."

And a soul eater, my mind whispered. *Don't forget that little tidbit.*

"I don't know how to not kill someone. It's one thing to be around lowlifes and monsters day in and day out. I don't know—I don't want to hurt anyone that doesn't deserve it."

Thomas snorted as he settled back in his seat. "Oh, I think the answer to that will arrive in three, two, one…"

At the end of Thomas' counting, Emrys' office door flew open with Sparky on the other side.

In his hand was a ball of electricity, and on his face was an expression of pure murder.

I was screwed.

8

Power crackled on the air, racing across my skin like ants as I contemplated just how fucked my current situation was. I fully expected Sparky to lob that ball of awful at me at his earliest convenience, but he never got the chance.

Emrys stood from behind her desk, batting her glowing palm at him like she was a pissed-off mama cat. Instantly, the ball of electricity in Bastian's hand fizzled and died, the scent of ozone and spent magic high on the air.

Mental note: Do not mess with Emrys. Ever.

Her expression seemed to be carved from stone, three times as rigid and twice as cold. "You called it, Thomas. It looks like we have a volunteer."

"Volunteer for what?" Bastian growled at the same

time I squeaked out a "What?"

I shook my head hard. I'd already smelled his blood. I'd already had to force myself not to attack him. If I sank my fangs into his skin...

I swallowed down the saliva gathering in my mouth, hunger wrenching in my belly. Already my fangs had lengthened, and it was all I could do to hold myself in the leather chair. My nails made little half-moon crescent slices in the leather as I physically restrained myself from launching at his neck and ripping it wide.

My heart tripped in my chest as he took a step inside the room.

"Get him out of here," I growled, my whole body vibrating with the urge to bathe in the warm, succulent bliss trapped in his veins. "I'll kill him. *Please.*"

Tears gathered in my eyes as my stomach twisted again, the hunger a burning agony of need.

It had been months since I'd gone more than twenty-four hours without feeding. After Jacob, I hadn't wanted to feed again—the horror of what I'd done, who I was, too much for me to understand. I had lost my parents, my life, my home. And I was a monster.

I didn't want to be a monster.

But the hunger was too much, and I was too new. The first arcaner I found was feasting on a woman's heart in the back room of a warehouse, the still-warm body of his meal crumpled at his feet. At the time I had no idea, but I now knew the man was a lycanthrope. I tore him apart, drank him down, and ate his soul.

It was the first time I wasn't sorry for killing, and the more arcaners I found in the recesses of Ascension, the less sorry I felt.

But if I killed Sparky, I was pretty sure I'd be sorry. The thought of the lycanthrope's flayed body flashed in my mind, and I shook my head again, my gaze pleading as the tears crested my lids and fell.

"I'll kill him," I whispered, begging now that I knew Emrys meant business.

Thomas knelt at my knees, a faint trace of empathy on his face for a split second before the condescending mask fell back into place. "You won't kill him. I'll be here to teach you. I can't have one of my line murdering arcaners left and right, now can I? If you look like you're taking too much, I'll stop you."

I was under no illusion that his version of "stopping" wouldn't hurt, but if it meant I wouldn't...

"You want to let her feed on me? What the fuck, Emrys?" Bastian growled, the rage in his voice palpable on the air.

"It's your penance for attacking her in the holding area, not to mention your insipid tantrum in my office not a moment ago. I gave you a job to do, and you failed.

Miserably. You deliberately went against my orders down there and continue to do so with every single bumbling, rage-filled misstep since I brought her here."

Bastian rocked back on his heels like he'd been slapped. While it was nice for Emrys to stick up for me, I had an inkling why Bastian wanted me gone. Given the way I was holding myself in my seat so I didn't rip his throat out, he'd have to be an idiot not to.

I was a threat to his brother, the last bit of family he had. He knew it. I knew it. We all knew why he was losing his shit like a tantrum-throwing toddler.

And I couldn't blame him. Not one bit.

Still, his reply burned me up from the inside. "She shouldn't be here. She doesn't belong with us."

"Yes, because everyone in this house has such a sparkling reputation?" Thomas quipped, the whites of his sclera veining red as he let his fangs descend.

"I'm not—" Bastian began, but Thomas cut him off.

"Do *not* lie. She is no different than any of us. Even you. And she needs to know how to feed so she is not a danger to you or your brother or anyone else in this house. Shall I ask Simon to volunteer instead?"

Bastian moved forward like he would attack but seemed to think better of it. Appearing to steal himself, he dropped his gaze to me. "I do this, you stay away from my brother."

"No," Emrys whispered, the single word like a barbed threat. "She will be a member of our house. She will dine with us—she will fight with us. You and your fears will not stand in the way of that."

Bastian's jaw hardened enough that I worried for the state of his teeth—or at least I would have had I not caught sight of the fluttering pulse just underneath it. This close, I could smell the drops of dried blood he still hadn't cleaned from his body, but that was nothing close to the scent of the rich lifeblood racing in his veins.

"Fine. If I do this, she cannot feed from anyone else. Not Simon, not Dahlia, or Harper. Just me. Deal?"

Dear sweet mother of all that was holy. Couldn't they just give me a bag of blood or something? I'd rather raid a blood bank than do this.

"Excellent," Thomas purred, a cat that got the canary smile blooming across his lips, putting his previous wicked grin to shame. "Come here, then. I have a feeling if she gets out of this chair, she'll rip your throat out."

That image bounced around my brain, and I winced at the truth of it.

With reluctance in his stride, Bastian approached my chair, kneeling at my feet. I sat there frozen until he smacked the side of my thigh with the back of his hand.

Oh. *Oh*. He meant for me to... Swallowing hard, I widened my legs, and he moved his big body in between them. It was all I could do to not lunge at his throat, but just before I lost what little bit of control I had, Thomas' iron grip landed on my shoulders.

"Some elders believe that a young one should always go for the wrist at first, but I disagree. It is far too easy to rip the delicate skin of a wrist, causing irreparable tendon damage. The throat, however, has a stronger pulse point, meaning it is far easier to feel the slowing of blood flow. Now"—He paused, letting his grip tighten on my shoulders—"you will stop when I tell you to. Understand?"

"I'll do my best," I whispered, unable to let my gaze stray too far from the pounding pulse in Bastian's throat.

"Comforting," Bastian muttered, moving closer as he latched his hands over my forearms on the armrest, pinning them to the seat.

Any other time, I would have balked at being held down, but if I were going to put my fangs in Bastian's neck, I figured I needed the restraint.

"Bite around the jugular, not through it. Yes?" Thomas advised, and I gave him a cursory sort of nod.

And then I struck, unable to hold back for another second as the hunger and heat and scent bombarded me like a battering ram. My razor-sharp fangs pierced Bastian's throat so fast he cried out. By some sort of miracle,

I managed not to bite all the way through, stopping just shy of his jugular.

Hot blood filled my mouth, the heady rich nectar flowing down my throat like the sweetest wine. I swallowed once more, letting the power of it fill me, heal me. How had I not noticed when my throat felt like sandpaper? How had I ignored the ache in my joints or the lethargy that filled my limbs? How had I not noticed until all those aches were wiped away, the blood healing so much so quickly. I'd never felt power like this, never drank blood so potent, so strong.

I swallowed again, my hands sneaking out of Bastian's hold. The fingers of one hand threaded through his hair and the other gripped his shirt, pulling him closer to me as I drank more. A scent I didn't recognize rose in the air, intoxicatingly sweet, incredibly potent. I wanted to roll in it like a cat in catnip, but all too quickly that thought was dashed. Because just like they always did, the images came.

Maybe because I wasn't drinking him dry, maybe because I didn't want to see Bastian's private thoughts and deeds, I didn't see everything like I always had. Instead, I saw flashes, just quick glimpses so fast I almost couldn't make them out. Flashes of... me?

Before I could see anymore, Thomas' grip tightened on my shoulders. Had they been there this whole time?

"It's time to stop, Sloane," Thomas called, his voice seeming so far away even though he couldn't be more than inches from me.

Reluctantly, I pulled my fangs back, wishing I could have more but knowing I couldn't. Only after my fangs had retracted from Bastian's throat did the world turn back on, and I realized the precarious situation I was now in.

Yes, in the time since my fangs pierced Bastian's flesh, my hands found their way to his hair and shirt, but moreover? Bastian's grip was also latched onto me. One of his arms was banded around my back, and the other hand had a full grip on my ass. And he wasn't moving.

Bastian's head rested on my chest, his breathing heavy like he'd run a marathon.

"Lick the wounds," Thomas instructed, and I whipped my head up to stare at him, his wicked grin wide as ever. "I'm serious. It will help the blood clot faster."

I tilted my head back down, my gaze latching onto the eight drops of blood that welled from the puncture wounds. They trickled down his neck, almost meeting the soft cotton of his shirt. Before I thought better of it, I flicked my tongue at the drops, sweeping them up as I passed over the wounds.

At the touch of my tongue, Bastian's grip got tighter, a faint shudder racking his big body. The faintest sort of groan slipped past his lips, and then I finally realized the scent coming from him—what it was.

Desire. Lust. Want.

Not that I understood it at all. Nor could I prevent the low clench inside me that answered the scent's siren call.

The quiet snick of the door closing meant I couldn't ask Thomas, either—not that I could ever see myself broaching the topic with the surly vampire—the room empty now that the danger of me killing Bastian was long gone. For the first time in a year, I wasn't hungry or thirsty, which didn't make any sense at all.

Was it because I had a willing victim?

Was it the strength in Bastian's blood?

And the thought of consuming his soul never once crossed my mind, which was another tick in the unexplainable column. Why did that satiate me before and not now? What was I missing?

We sat there for what seemed like a long time—me watching the wounds heal on his neck as I pondered, and Bastian holding onto me like a barnacle, his breathing slowing by small increments.

It probably should have been awkward, but I was riding high on the bliss of my joints not hurting, my whole body not aching, and the buzzing thoughts pinging around my skull.

Plus... I hadn't hugged anyone in a very long time. It felt almost... nice. That wasn't the right word, but it was as close as I would let myself get.

Bastian rolled his head, his breathing finally slowed enough for him to pull away. His fingers seemed reluctant to pull themselves from my ass cheek. Same with his arm. It was almost as if he didn't want to let me go.

There had to be something with the bite. Maybe I was venomous or something. Yeah, that was totally possible.

But then he shifted away, the loss of his heat leaving me chilled all over as he stood. He moved to walk away and abruptly stopped.

I glanced up, reluctant to see whatever censure or hate or disgust he was going to shovel my way. This was the first time I felt okay in a year and he was going to ruin it.

But instead of censure, all I saw was a carefully constructed blank mask, save for his eyes flashing emerald. "No one else," he rumbled, his voice shattering the quiet. "Only me."

Then he walked out of the room, leaving me to wonder what the hell had just happened.

9

It took far too long to collect myself after Bastian left the room. I had to wonder when I stopped calling him Sparky. Was it when I dug my fangs into his neck that his moniker changed? And what was the deal with the "only me" shit?

Not that I had plans to strike on any other member of the house, but...

My mind replayed the words over and over. *Only me.* Each time, my belly dipped—each time, Bastian's blood thundered through my veins. I was hovering on the edge of hunting him down to ask him what the fuck was going on or hiding from him until the end of time.

Why was I so embarrassed? I was twenty-three not thirteen, and I hadn't exactly been a saint before my world had gone promptly to shit. So why was I acting like a blushing virgin?

Ugh. I'd have to ask Thomas, and I really didn't want to. He'd make fun of me at every turn, but dammit, I needed answers. And at least with Thomas I knew what I was going to get. If I asked Bastian, I had no idea what he'd do. Lash out? Kiss me? Ask me to bite him again?

I threw my arms over my head, hiding my face from the empty room. The scent of Bastian's need was still high on the air and no matter how much I wanted to talk myself out of it, the urge to fill my lungs with it was strong. I had to get the fuck out of here before I did something really stupid.

I shoved myself up from the chair and stalked out of the room, the fresh air of the hall slamming me in the face. It was cooler, the scents of the house less heady and intoxicating. I missed his smell already. How stupid was that? So was the urge to follow his scent down the hall.

My hand still on the doorknob, I stepped back into Emrys' office to get one last breath of him before I shut that nagging urge down. What the fuck was wrong with me? Wasn't I the same girl who spiked his head like a volleyball an hour ago?

Suddenly, a door whipped open, and Harper's

scowling face peeked out of the opening. "I thought I told you to get warded?"

"Sorry. Shenanigans ensued, and..." I shrugged by way of answer. "I'll find Emrys and get it done." The thought of what she might be gleaning from me made my face heat with embarrassment. "Sorry," I muttered again, inexplicable tears gathering in my eyes.

The unholy rage left her face for a moment. "It's fine. *You're* fine. Just get it done. This is supposed to be a safe place for me. There aren't many left for people like me anymore."

I did my absolute best not to feel pity—Harper didn't need it and didn't deserve it. What she needed was my respect. I could give her that. "I'll get it done."

"Good." She moved from behind her door to lean on the doorjamb. "And afterward, you can dish about whatever happened in that office, because, *girl*. Whatever went down was hot as *hell*."

My face felt like the surface of the sun. Dear sweet mother, I was not going to talk about that shit. Maybe ever.

"Oh, my god, your face! I had no idea vampires could blush." And then she giggled—the girl who had been nothing but surly since I got here was giggling like a schoolgirl.

Someone shoot me.

I opened my mouth to tell her I wasn't a vampire but immediately snapped it shut. That was information I didn't need to bandy about. Instead, I narrowed my eyes at her and stuck out my tongue. It wasn't her fault she felt that shit, but damn, was tact taboo in this place or what?

"I'm finding Emrys to put the whammy on me, and then... we can never discuss this shit ever again. Nice to meet you, Harper," I called over my shoulder as I hauled ass down the hall and down the stairs.

Following the sounds of voices, I found an opulent dining space off the great room. A wide chandelier made from several globe lights hung in the middle of a giant table, the thing long enough to seat twenty.

While the majority of the house was more of a traditional style, the dining room was more contemporary. A slate-gray rug lay under the table, the thick pile close to a trendy shag. I never understood how to keep shag rugs clean, but damn, did it look soft.

Emrys and Thomas were off in a corner discussing things I wanted no part of. Still, I approached, ready for Harper to never know another thing about my emotions, ever.

"Done already?" Thomas teased. He was quickly rewarded with my face likely turning tomato red—I'd felt the heat as it immediately crept up my cheeks. He had to have smelled Bastian's desire just like I did, only he knew what it was as soon as it happened. Me, not so much.

"Was I supposed to drain him dry in your absence?" I immediately wished I hadn't asked the question as soon as it fell out of my mouth. Double entendre had never been my strong suit, but I figured Thomas had been around when that shit was invented. As strong as he was, he had to be older than dirt.

Thomas' smile stretched wide. "In a manner of speaking. What do you need?"

Deciding to ignore his dig, I explained the issue. "Harper said I was supposed to be warded? And considering she's yelled at me three times already, I'd like that to be done now-ish if possible."

Emrys' lips tipped up like she knew exactly why I wanted the ward so damn bad. Good god, did everyone in the house know what happened when I drank Bastian's blood?

"Of course. My apologies. In all the commotion, it slipped my mind. Stay still," she instructed, waving a glowing hand in my face before she touched two fingers to my chest.

I felt only warmth, but I heard Harper call a resounding "thank you" across the house so I figured it worked. I wanted to be relieved, wanted to bask in the warmth of having my emotions known only to myself, but then Bastian strode in the room, and I became a ball of I had no idea what. I was a tangled yarn of weird emotions, and I didn't like it one bit.

Emotions sucked.

Big time.

Bastian's neck was completely healed, the skin smooth and unblemished. There wasn't even a scar. I couldn't detect the faintest hint of blood either, not even the old blood that he'd failed to clean off his boots from before. Then I noticed his wet hair, and it dawned on me that he must have showered, washing my scent away while I was busy trying to keep his in my nose.

I couldn't say exactly why this felt like a slap in the face, but it did. My only solace was at least that information was mine alone and not for public consumption. The absolute last thing I needed right that second was some asshole to tell me that I was blushing, or looked hurt, or whatever.

Maybe I was just tired. Right. The sun was just cresting the horizon—or at least that's what my internal clock said. I could blame all this emotional bullshit on that. Except I'd never been so energized in my life, Bastian's blood filling me, nourishing me.

I nearly groaned out loud but managed to stop

myself. Still, I got a knowing glance from Thomas who could likely smell my freak-out leaking from my pores.

Fabulous.

"Are you going to eat breakfast with us?" Dahlia's said from my elbow, and I nearly jumped out of my skin. I could have sworn she appeared out of nowhere. "I promise it isn't poisoned."

"I don't know."

Dahlia grabbed my elbow, yanking me to a seat with way more force than a woman that small should have. "You have to. Whenever we aren't on assignment, we always eat one meal together. Granted, we're on assignment so much it's ridiculous, but still. It's been a month since we were able to have a meal together. Even Harper is coming down. Now, Booth and Axel are out of pocket, so you won't get to meet them yet, but it'll be fun."

She practically shoved me into a seat and plopped down beside me.

"Oo-kay. I guess I'll stay."

Dahlia clapped. "You won't regret it. Clementine is the best cook in the state. Makes pancakes made of magic. Fluffy clouds of awesome that just melt in your mouth. Really. You're in for a treat. It feels like forever since we all got to sit down together."

I didn't see any food on the table, but I was willing to wait and see what all the fuss was about. I mean, who could turn down pancakes? Especially ones described with such reverence. It had been a very long time since I'd gotten anything close to a home-cooked meal.

No, Cup O' Noodles did not count, no matter how good they were.

Simon fell onto the chair to my left, and Bastian yanked out the one across from him, slamming onto the seat with a roughness that likely heralded another temper tantrum. Good god, couldn't that man maintain an emotion for more than thirty seconds?

"I need to talk to you," Simon said under his breath, a faint whisper I knew no one but me and Thomas could hear.

I looked down rather than meeting his eyes. "About?"

"My brother, doofus. What do you think?" he hissed back, and I could see his ridged shoulders out of the corner of my eye.

"If he doesn't haul across the table and murder me, sure. I'll pencil you in."

"You'd better." Simon's tone was so different than the one he'd used before. Like I had injured him some-how. I couldn't tell what I had done from then to now that could cause such a fuss except...

Again, I wanted to groan but didn't. Damn Thomas

and Emrys for making Bastian feed me. What had they been thinking?

A pretty young woman in a polka-dotted fifties-style house dress swept in from a swinging door, the opening giving a slight glimpse of a kitchen before it swung shut. In her hands were two trays loaded with several serving dishes, and despite how heavy they looked, she appeared to carry them with ease. Her blood-red hair was carefully coiffed into victory rolls, her eyeliner sharp enough to cut steal. On her feet were a pair of heels I would have broken my neck in and save for the fact that she was most certainly not alive, I kind of wished I could take style tips from her.

And by not alive, I meant that her pallor was paler than a ghost, her eyes and the hollows of her cheeks carrying deep shadows, and her head was most definitely stitched on.

What was she, Bride of freaking Frankenstein?

Dahlia answered my unspoken question, whispering in my ear, "She's a revenant. A nice one, but she's still a ghost shoved into a reanimated body. She used to be a dybbuk, but Simon helped expel her. It was a whole thing. She didn't want to move on, so Simon put her in that body, and she works for us."

Dahlia was the queen of information, but I still had questions. "Dybbuk? What the hell is that?"

She put her finger to her lips, shushing me. "It's a possessing spirit. Usually they need help, have unfinished business, so they jump into someone's body. In Clem's case, she jumped into Booth, which was so wrong on every level." She shuddered. "Anyway, that's a story for another time."

What I wouldn't give to ply Dahlia with alcohol and let her spill all the dirt hiding out in her brain.

A clinking glass pulled my gaze from Dahlia to Emrys who stood at the head of the table. "Before we dig in, I have a few announcements. Everyone, welcome our newest member, Sloane. For the time being, I will be partnering her with Simon—"

Even though I was expecting it, I still jumped when Bastian's fists slammed against the table.

"Absolutely not."

10

"I was unaware you were in charge here, Mr. Cartwright," Emrys said, her tone coy, but I still caught the faint thread of threat buried under guile. "Should you be at the head of this table then?"

Bastian stood from his seat, his fists pressed against the wood like he was drawing from the planks. "We all know by now that she is a blood drinker."

Thanks for blurting it out for everyone to hear, Sparky.

"If she's partnered with Simon, what happens when she's injured and needs blood to heal? Or when they're on assignment so long she requires a meal? We discussed that I would be the only person to feed her in this house. If she's going to be partnered with anyone, it should be me."

Out of the two brothers, I would have much

preferred to be paired with Simon. For one, I wouldn't be worried about random outbursts. The second reason —and likely more pressing of the two—feeding from Bastian wasn't an experience I wanted to duplicate. It felt dangerous in a way that had the potential for catastrophic consequences.

And he wanted to be partners? Was he high? Other than the blip of him hugging me mid-feeding, Bastian couldn't stand me. He was more likely to stab me in my sleep than be a good partner—not that I'd ever had a partner for anything other than a school project, but still. It wasn't rocket science.

Emrys' silence stretched long enough that I spared her a glance to see if she was preparing to blast Sparky to kingdom come. Her face was a blank mask—a look that was not comforting at all. "So, I can trust you to actually be Sloane's partner, and not treat her like shit on your shoe? I can trust you to feed her when she is injured or in need? I can have faith that you will actually utilize her gifts instead of benching her because of your attitude? If you can promise me that, then absolutely, it makes sense for the two of you to be partners. If you can't, then she needs to pair up with someone who isn't the embodiment of a—what did you call it, Harper?"

Harper entered the room, taking her seat next to Bastian, a malevolent smirk on her elfin face. "A butthurt diaper baby with little dick syndrome." She happily reached for one of the still-covered platters. To Bastian, she said, "Sack up, dude."

The table erupted into peals of laughter. Even Emrys and Thomas let out a giggle, but the most surprising was Bastian's booming laugh as he plopped back onto his seat. He laughed until he had tears coming from his eyes, the smile on his face wholly unexpected.

They teased each other like a family—just like mine did before...

I did not laugh—I couldn't. Despite the mirth in the room, I waited for the other shoe to drop, waited for someone to kick me out or tell me I wasn't wanted or that I didn't belong here. Yes, Emrys was sticking up for me, but that seemed like more of a dig at Thomas and Bastian and less for my benefit.

Or maybe I was just looking for ways to sabotage what little hope I had. If I didn't have a home, I couldn't lose one. If I didn't have friends, they couldn't die on me. If I didn't have hope, I wouldn't be crushed when everything inevitably went to shit.

All of this played out undetected from Harper's empath abilities, a fact for which I was supremely grateful. Casting my gaze downward, I hid my face from the rest of the table. I wanted to look at Bastian, wanted to see what was going on behind his eyes, but I couldn't make myself be a part of this hodge-podge family.

"Well, if the state of my manhood is at stake," Bastian rumbled, "I suppose I will just have to rise to the challenge."

Good. This was good. I shouldn't get comfortable here. I shouldn't stick with people who would become fast friends.

I was a killer, wasn't I? Even if I killed bad people, Bastian was right not to want me around his little brother. Killers didn't get friends. Killers didn't get happy families and warm meals and cushy digs and...

Abruptly, I stood, my chair snagging on the shag rug and tipping back in my haste to leave. The crack of it hitting the floor didn't slow me down one bit, and even though the door was easily accessible, and I knew I could leave, I didn't. Instead, I found myself back in my cell, the small quarters somehow more comforting than any other place I'd visited. Without a thought in my head, I pulled the cell door closed.

The runes began to glow as soon as the metal slammed home, the magic locks springing closed. The heat seeped into my palm, and I let the metal go before it could burn me. I couldn't say why that made me breathe easier, being locked in this cell. I couldn't say why I wanted the barrier, but I did. I wanted something to separate me from them. Wanted—no, needed—a way to keep myself away.

From the laughter. From the happiness. From the warmth.

My mom's face flashed in my head—she was smiling wide enough that her crooked canine was visible. She hardly ever smiled that wide because she hated that she'd never gotten braces. A silly thing that my father and I always got on her about when she hid her smile. We were giggling about a misadventure of our family dog, Otis. She'd taken him on a walk, and he'd rolled in the mud—only it wasn't mud but a pile of crap. And then—the big bastard that he was—knocked my mom in the same pile he'd just rolled in.

My mom was so pissed when she began the story, but by the end, my dad and I were out of our chairs laughing at my mom's tale of woe, tears spilling from our eyes. And poor Otis didn't know which human he wanted to inspect because Dad and I were making such a ruckus.

That was two days before the death date on my—*our*—tombstones.

It was the last thing I remembered from before. The last memory I had of my parents, of Otis. Of my home. The last thing I remembered before waking up in the dirt of that stupid cemetery.

. . .

Smoke filled my nose as I crawled on my bedroom floor to the window. My skin felt like it was melting off my bones. I reached for the window, but it was too far away. Too far…

My mother's scream pierced the air, the pain reaching my ears as she called my name.

A clanging on metal had my eyes flashing open, my body up and off the cot in an instant. I found myself crouched low to the ground, a feral sort of growl ripping up my throat, the remnant of the dream still at the forefront of my mind.

Bastian stood on the other side of the bars, his large body appearing that much bigger since I was on the floor.

"Remind me never to wake you up when you're in your actual bed. Care to share why you chose the dungeon instead of your room?"

Reluctantly, I stood from my crouch. "Room? I thought this was my room."

"No, members of the Watch do not sleep in the dungeon. Why would you think that?"

My gaze landed on the charcoals, the box a stark reminder of the life I'd lost, and the reason I thought I was supposed to stay down here.

"Do you like them?" His question was reluctant, like

he was trying desperately to make conversation. "It was difficult to find anything on you. Neither you nor your parents had any social media to speak of. The only thing I found of any note was a picture of you in a university art class with a box of those. Dahlia said that they might make you feel at home. Reassure you that we weren't the bad guys."

"And all they did was make me angry," I whispered, blinking hard so I didn't start crying. Every time I closed my eyes, I saw the fire racing over the walls of my bedroom. Was that a memory? Or was it just my imagination running wild?

I didn't know, and it was driving me crazy.

"My mom got me a set when I was young. I was saving for them, but they were ridiculously expensive." I shook my head, unable to explain why that box made me want to scream.

"She sounds like a good mum."

My smile was brittle, but I managed to answer him without crying. "She was. She was the best. A little over-protective and overbearing, but dammit, she was a great mom."

"And your dad?"

Mom, I could think about, but Dad was like a knife in the gut every time. Still, I answered, even though my voice was little more than a croak. "The best."

Bastian sat in the chair across from the bars. "Do you know what happened?"

I swiped at my cheeks and nose. "Nope. One day I was living my best life, worried about classes and whether or not I could convince Mom to let me apply for the Fine Arts master's program, and the next, I'm in that fucking cemetery staring at our headstones."

"We all have stories like yours, you know?" His words weren't mean, in fact, they were likely meant to be reassuring. "People we've lost. Wrongs done to us. Bitter wounds that refuse to heal. Thomas was right yesterday. We're not so different."

I stared at my feet rather than meet his gaze. He was right—these people likely had just as much pain as I did. Why else would they be here instead of with a family? Why would they be bounty hunters instead of something else?

"You're probably right."

"As long as you keep that attitude, we'll get along just fine." With a wave of his hands, he completed a set of hand movements similar to Dahlia's, unlocking my cell. "Time for training. Booth and Axel are back, so you're about to be put through the wringer."

Groaning, I shoved my feet into my boots, exiting the cell with the exact same wariness I had yesterday. The difference was, he didn't pounce. I glanced over my shoulder, giving him a steely-eyed glare. "No attacking today?"

Bastian chuckled. "There will be plenty of that in training. First, I'll show you to your room. You can get cleaned up and then we'll head to the gym. If we're going to work together, we'll need to see how we mesh as a combat team. I don't take the easy cases."

"I've kicked your ass how many times in a twenty-four-hour period?" I prodded, letting him lead the way with the added benefit of not being attacked from behind.

"Twice, if you're keeping score, but I was being gentle. You were a capture job, not a kill."

I snorted. *The ego on this guy.* "Doesn't explain the dungeon attack. You got bested. Twice. Admit it."

"We'll see how much you're crowing after training. Booth has been instructed by Thomas to go full-bore. Your *sire* really is concerned about your fighting abilities. Seems his first impression of you was a bit... *lacking.*"

That sounded like Thomas all right. The surly vampire was desperate to be a verified pain in my ass.

Which was why—after a shower and a cursory glance at the ridiculously spacious room they gave me—I ended up face-to-face with the business end of a shifter's fangs.

11

Bastian led me up the set of stairs to the main level and up the grand staircase to the second floor. My feet practically sank into the plush carpet on the stairs, the feeling still odd to me even after my trek on them the day before. My senses felt funny, slightly amped up, and I had to wonder if it was Bastian's feeding that dialed them to eleven.

To the right was the long corridor that led to Simon's room, ahead was a small alcove with Harper's domain, and to the left was Emrys' office. In between the doorways were tiny insets with vases or portraits, but the largest was a painted portrait of a woman in a red dress. The picture was so large, it was a wonder I missed it yesterday.

I paused slightly, studying it. The brunette woman

possessed an unearthly level of beauty, her hair coiffed in glam waves of a 1940s movie star, her face turned in profile as she stared off into the distance. Her skin was flawless alabaster, save for a sprinkling of freckles peppering her nose. Her dress floated around her like a cloud, but it wasn't just her hair or skin or dress. It was her eyes, the whiskey color almost bright against her skin. The portrait was done by an expert hand, the colors flowing beautifully together to make her skin almost glow. There was no artist signature at the bottom, which irked me to no end.

Bastian turned right, his gaze directed from the portrait—seemingly on purpose—as he forged down the hall, his face veered away until he'd moved past it.

Was she someone he had lost, someone he hated? Bastian was so closed off, I'd probably never know.

Simon's room was at the end of the corridor, and Bastian stopped three rooms away, opening the heavily carved wood door with a practiced ease. I reluctantly followed only to have my jaw drop once he stepped aside. The walls were a deep teal, the color so rich it almost hurt my heart. At the center of the room was an upholstered king-size bed, the blush-velvet headboard striking against the color of the wall. Dangling above the bed was a brushed-gold geometric chandelier that seemed delicate and modern and made my little artist heart sing. Off to the side, near the giant picture window was an easel with a blank canvas, a drafting table, and a brushed-gold, pin-leg stool with a velvet teal cushion.

"Please tell me you like it?" Dahlia begged, her tiny body shoving Bastian out of the way so she could give me a side-armed hug. "Thomas said artists need the best light, so I switched with you. This room is a little smaller than my new one, but it has a giant window and a fireplace.

This room has a fireplace? My gaze had been so stuck on the art supplies that I missed the sleek hearth, the tile surrounding it reaching all the way to the ceiling.

"Your bathroom is to the right, and you can get to your closet through there." She pointed to a teal door with gold moldings. "I took the liberty of getting your wardrobe started. Just the basics. Emrys said you didn't have much in the way of things, so I wanted you to feel at home."

I swallowed hard, an emotion hitting me square in the chest that I didn't want to name. It was part pain, part happiness, part misery. It made me want to hug her and punch her in the face all at the same time. I settled on the hug, squeezing her gently so as to not break her tiny bones.

"Dammit, Dahlia," I croaked. "How am I supposed to

kick Bastian's ass for the third time if you keep doing nice shit like this?"

She giggled and hip-checked me with enough force that I figured her earlier bouts of helplessness had to be a ruse. "You'll figure out something else to be mad at. So, you like it? You haven't even looked at the bathroom yet."

"Does it have a working shower and toilet?"

She nodded.

"Then I'll love it." I'd been squatting in warehouses and slums for the last year. If the bathroom looked anything like this sort of opulence, I was going to be just fine.

"You say that now, but it doesn't have a soaking tub. I tried to get Booth to put one in, but he said the old plumbing wouldn't support another water line without *blah, blah, blah.* Which really meant he didn't want to do it and figured out a way to bullshit me into accepting the shower-only option. But my new room has the mother of all tubs, and I cannot wait!"

"So what you're really saying is the move was a total sacrifice, but you did it for me because you owe me like a Wookie life-debt or something," I deadpanned, watching as her smile grew wider.

Dahlia put her hand over her heart like she was reciting the Pledge of Allegiance. "Exactly. Total sacrifice. I don't know how I'll live with it, but I will. For you."

"Fabulous," Bastian drawled. "Get cleaned up and meet me in the gym in an hour. Booth will want to assess your strength before we start." With that, he turned and left, his abrupt departure raising both my and Dahlia's eyebrows.

"That boy needs to get laid. I swear, he gets crankier every day," she muttered, shaking her head. "Here, I'll show you were you get new clothes." She stalked off to the closet, and immediately got to work yanking out underwear and a sports bra, activewear and shoes. "Typically, we train in what we fight in, but if Booth wants to assess you, then he's about to put you through the wringer. Basically, it's going to be a free-for-all to see if you can lift as heavy or do as many push-ups as he can. Comfort is key. Trust me."

Goodie.

After a shower in the biggest freaking bathroom I had ever seen, I donned my new clothes. It had been a long time since something I wore was new or clean or without holes. I was reluctant to leave my leather pants behind, though. I'd stolen them fair and square, and they were still in good shape after a year of hard use.

"Here." Dahlia held her hand out. "I'll have Clem clean them. You'd think it was a chore, but I swear, that woman loves to do laundry. I've never met anyone who loves to fold more than her."

Reluctantly, I handed over the leather, the feeling of it parting from my hands leaving me bereft. I'd washed off what felt like a year's worth of dirt and blood and grime. I felt clean for the first time in a while. Even though I'd done what I could to stay clean, squatting in warehouses hadn't been the best means in which to stay that way. But I'd had little choice. *So, there's that.*

"She'll give them back, I promise. You aren't the only one with an attachment to the old life. When Emrys found me, I'd been eating out of the garbage for six months. There weren't a lot of safe places for witches back then. But our population has grown quite a bit over the last century. Less burnings and trials, I'd bet."

I blinked hard. "How old are you?"

Dahlia swept her braids off her shoulder. "Don't you know you're not supposed to ask a woman that?" she teased. "I was born in 1909. Witches don't typically age as well as I do, but I'm pretty sure I have a little mage blood mixed in there." She said it behind her hand like it was a big secret. "Super taboo back then, not that I know who my parents even are. I was left on the steps of an orphanage as a baby, and those nuns kicked me out the second I displayed an inkling of magic. I lived on the streets until Emrys found me, and I've been here ever since."

I suddenly didn't feel so bad about handing over my leather pants. Scanning the room, I noticed all the little details she'd put into it to make me feel at home, to make it so I would stay. From the bed, to the art table, to the color on the walls. The scent still clung on the air, meaning she'd chosen that color for me, decorating the space exactly like I would want it.

"Thanks," I rasped, trying not to burst into tears at the generosity. Really, I was going to have to punch someone in the face or snap someone's neck to get all these gooey, happy feelings out of me.

"Don't worry about it." She shrugged, heading for the door. "They all did the same for me when I got here. Except for Simon. He only let me into his room, but that was enough. He was dealing with a lot back then. Speak of the devil..." She trailed off as Simon leaned against the doorjamb.

"And he appears," he answered. "Do you mind if I talk to Sloane for a bit?"

"Show her how to get to the gym, would you? I have to read the cards and put some hex bags together." Dahlia yanked his sleeve, and he leaned down. She gave him a raspberry on his cheek before flouncing out of the room, the trails of her bouncy skirt following behind her.

For some reason, I braced myself. Simon wanted to talk to me yesterday, but I'd bounced out of breakfast like a melodramatic teenager. I wasn't all too eager to find out what he wanted to say, but it seemed like my time was up.

Simon pressed on the bridge of his glasses, sliding them up his nose. He adjusted his beanie and fiddled with the cuffs of his flannel shirt. The scent of reluctance wafted toward me, mixed with spent magic and a little fear.

"Out with it," I growled, irritated at his stalling. "If you're going to shatter my happy bubble, at least have the decency to quit stalling, Simon. It's rude."

He opened his mouth to begin, but closed it, his expression just as frustrated as mine likely was.

"You didn't even bring your cat, and to think I was counting on that as a perk of our friendship."

Simon chuckled before sobering. "This is going to sound all kinds of wrong, but if I don't say it, I'll regret it. Just know what I'm about to say has nothing to do with you as a person, and everything to do with my bonehead brother and his fragile, stupid heart."

Oh, I did not like where this was going.

"Don't start with him. Be partners, be friends. Don't

start a relationship with him. You think it will work, but it won't. And if you get hurt, if you die on him, he'll..." Simon shook his head, covering his bespectacled face with his hands. "I'm not explaining this right."

"It's okay, man. I don't think your brother likes me, anyway. And he's cute and all—if you like hot, broody, magic-wielding dolts who don't look before they leap."

Simon peeked from between his fingers. "I am messing this up royally. Okay, so if we could get back to the issue here."

"Which is don't diddle your brother."

"Exactly. Blood drinkers have a way of... charming their sources. Especially if they are a repeat. The more you bite him, the more he'll want to be bitten. The more he'll want you. It's sort of a symbiotic relationship, only it usually involves..."

"Sex?" I wasn't an idiot. I was smart enough to put two and two together. My bite made a normally rage-filled mage into a possessive behemoth with a penchant for grabbing my ass. It didn't mean it had to progress beyond that, right?

Simon blushed so hard the lobes of his ears turned scarlet. Dahlia was over a century old, and Simon had been here since before she had. That meant he was ancient compared to me and blushing like a virgin on prom night.

"Look, I've fed from him once. How about I do blood bags from now on, and we'll see if the attraction fades. If it does, no harm, no foul." I didn't say what would happen if it didn't. Because the both of us had no idea.

Simon reluctantly ended the conversation, his purpose muddied with worry for his brother and his awkwardness about the subject matter. He silently led me to the gym, gave me a mumbled goodbye, and practically sprinted for the stairs.

The wide-open room boasted a climbing wall, tons of weightlifting equipment, and all the accoutrement of a well-stocked gym. A stocky man in a singlet and shorts approached, his hands rubbing together like he was hatching a Machiavellian plan. His long blond hair was pulled into a knot at the top of his head, and I couldn't say why that irritated me, but it did.

I also didn't like the glint to his eyes, or the way his mouth twisted up at the corner, nor was I a fan of the scent of his magic. It smelled of untamed wildness and malice.

He held out one of his beefy hands for me to shake, and stupidly, I took it, assuming that introductions were safe. Booth yanked me to him in a move that was likely intended to dump me on my ass. A fact that was proved correct not a moment later when I was tossed up and over his hip.

Too bad for Booth, landing on my feet was a specialty. So was hitting back. Sailing over his hip, I latched onto his singlet, bringing the fabric up to wrap around his neck. In less than a second, Booth was being choked out by his own shirt, while I yawned dramatically.

Bastian sauntered toward our little tableau, clapping as he struggled to breathe from laughing so hard.

"You should have probably introduced yourself before acting like an asshole, Booth," Bastian advised once his chuckles subsided.

At Bastian's nod, I let Booth go, relishing the wheeze of him sucking in air.

"Hi, Booth. I'm Sloane. Nice to meet you." I said it like butter wouldn't melt in my mouth, trying for a guileless smile. I likely failed, but it really didn't matter. I had a feeling Booth and I weren't going to be friends.

"Pleasure," he wheezed back, on his hands and knees, his hair escaping the tie and hiding his face.

Bastian knelt by his friend, slapping him on the back. "I told you not to. As I recall, I also told you she would hand you your ass."

"Yeah, you did," Booth replied, getting to his feet. "But I had to see what this little lady was made of. I couldn't believe it when Emrys said who she was. I mean, two hundred arcaners? By this little thing? It had to be bullshit."

"Yeah, I'm standing right here," I growled, irritated to no end that the man was talking about me like I wasn't there. "And it's three hundred."

Booth's gaze shifted to me, the glint in his eyes reminding me of Jacob for a split second. "Oh, is it now? Well, I guess we'll just have to see if you can handle a real opponent then."

12

I was going to kill Thomas. I would drink him down and eat his soul and watch gleefully as he withered to dust.

Booth, the godforsaken shapeshifter who was in charge of my training, was a certified sadist. A fact that was more and more evident the longer my training went on. The first thirty minutes, I was cursing Booth, but I'd since shifted my ire onto Thomas. Booth might be an asshole, but he was the weapon Thomas was wielding, and I was going to get my revenge on him someday.

Booth's razor-sharp fangs snapped, barely missing my arm by millimeters. Since he was so close, I latched onto his thick white fur and launched him across the room, hoping he hit his stupid thick head and passed out. It had been wishful thinking, but it was what I had.

At his returning growl, I figured I was shit out of luck. Especially since Booth wasn't the only person in this house I would be fighting. Bastian's low chuckle was faint enough that I'd be willing to bet he thought I couldn't hear him.

Rookie mistake.

Now I knew he was up in the catwalk area where the climbing ropes were secured, waiting to hit me when I was down. That's what this exercise was supposed to be —an assessment of my skills with more than one opponent. I refused to look up, so I didn't let on that I knew he was up there, keeping a wary eye on Booth instead.

"You think you're funny, but I assure you that if I could use *my* fangs, you'd be singing a different tune." Early in our training, Booth and Bastian informed me I couldn't use my best offensive weapon—a rule I thought was utterly unfair and a waste of time. If we were in a real battle, I was going to use anything I had at my disposal.

Including my teeth.

I felt the rise of magic on the air and smartly ducked. Not a moment later, a ball of fire whizzed by where my head *used* to be. *Rude.*

In the briefing before Bastian and Booth plotted new and inventive ways of kicking my ass, I'd also been informed that creating electricity balls was not Bastian's only talent. Oh, no. The bastard had control of a whole complement of elements.

I was dealing with an elemental mage and a shifter. And the fuckers were working in tandem because Booth decided to strike right when I was distracted, sinking his teeth into my forearm and shaking his head to rip the wound wide.

Motherfucker.

That was it, no more playing nice. Bastian, Booth, *and* Thomas could take their rules and shove them up their asses.

My fingers found Booth's muzzle, and I wrenched, the crack of his jaw breaking audible as I tore his teeth out of my arm. The limb now useless, I struggled to latch onto the damn dog, as he attempted to claw me to ribbons. But I was motivated and pissed right the fuck off. My fingers found his scruff and yanked, pulling him off his giant paws.

Booth was close to two hundred pounds as a human. As a wolf, he was slightly smaller, more compact. But it didn't matter if he were bigger, I'd had my fill of Bastian's blood the night before, so I had no trouble lifting him one-handed so I could stare into his stupid face.

I didn't know wolves could have a contemptuous expression on their furry faces, but Booth proved the rule. I had a feeling if he could close his mouth, my neck would be mincemeat.

"Be happy you will be nursing a broken jaw and not a broken fucking neck. Do. Not. Bite. Me. Again. Not unless you want me to bite you back. I've killed a lot of men for far less."

I was still holding Booth aloft when Bastian approached, a frown marring his pretty face. Well, too damn bad. I wasn't going to be bitten and not defend myself. No way.

"What the fuck did you do?" he thundered, and it was all I could do not to volley the damn wolf at him and watch them both fall like dominos.

"He bit me, so I broke his jaw." Why I needed to explain this was beyond me. "He's lucky I didn't break his stupid neck. How is this training, exactly?"

Bastian rolled his eyes. "Not you. Him. Booth, what in the bloody hell is wrong with you? Her arm is shredded."

I kinda figured that was the point of this bullshit training session—to make me bleed. I mean, not a second ago, Bastian was aiming an electricity ball at my nugget, so the goal couldn't have been to tiptoe through the fucking tulips.

I stared down at said arm. Blood ran down my finger-tips to puddle on the floor. I felt more than heard a faint displacement of air, quieter than a whoosh but louder than a breath, and then Thomas was looming over me, his sclera bled to scarlet as his needle-like fangs erupted from the periodontal pockets that held his secondary set of teeth.

His touch was cold as death as he gently took my injured forearm in his hands to examine the wounds.

"Drop the dog, Sloane." His voice was like ice, his gaze never moving from the weeping wounds.

Opening my fingers as instructed, I watched as Booth's limp body fell to the gym floor. Still conscious, the idiot was at least smart enough not to move. The cold finger of fear tickled down my back as Thomas' focus left my arm and landed on Booth.

"You were instructed to test her abilities. To see if she could handle multiple opponents, to see if she had any tactical skills. And although she proved she could best you, you decided on your own to injure her. On purpose and with intent." Thomas' words never rose above a whisper, but they chilled me to the bone. The rage wafting off of him soured the air, and although his ire was not directed at me, I still felt the cold breath of fear. Thomas was trying extremely hard not to murder someone, and I really didn't want it to be me.

"She is of my line, and as such, under my protection. Moreover, she is a member of this team. Your actions shall have consequences—not only with me, but with Emrys as well. I suggest you shift and heal your jaw. You will need to be at a hundred percent if you wish to survive your punishment."

A whine came from Booth's throat—it sounded confused, and I had to agree. None of this made much sense to me. Why was Thomas so angry? Why was a wall of rage coming from Bastian? Why was Booth being punished?

I wanted to ask, but it didn't feel right to. It felt like if I did, they would see just how out of place I felt, just how singular, and then they would try to bring me into the circle.

I couldn't say why that felt wrong, but it did.

"Sloane, if you wish to feed from Booth, you may." Thomas' voice was pitched so low, I could have sworn I misheard him. "He drew your blood—it is only right that you draw his."

"No." The answer did not come from me. Instead, that single barbed word came from Bastian's throat.

I swallowed hard, the pain finally registering now that the adrenaline was starting to wear off. "No, thank you."

Thomas shrugged as if both my and Bastian's refusal was of no consequence. "Bastian then? You will need healing."

This time it was me who emphatically vetoed that course of action. "If there's a blood bag or something, that would be fine."

I did not need a repeat of the last feeding I had with Bastian—didn't need him closer, especially given Simon's warning. That didn't stop me from meeting his knowing gaze. Nor did it hide the small bit of censure I found there. Did he want to be my personal Capri Sun? Or did he want something else?

"We keep an emergency stash of blood in the infirmary," Thomas answered. "If you wish to drink that swill, be my guest, just inform Axel of what you take so he can keep stocked."

Thomas turned to Bastian. "You will escort her there and stay until she is well again. If the blood does not heal her, you will. Do not presume that I am not holding you accountable for her injuries as well, Cartwright."

Bastian paled slightly, but gave Thomas a stiff nod before guiding me out of the impossibly big gym. Only when we were out of the double doors and down the hall did I broach what had plagued me since Thomas started talking.

"What was that?"

Bastian snorted. "That was Booth acting like the ultimate asshole."

"No, I got that. With Thomas, I mean. What the fuck was that?"

Bastian's steps stuttered—the action faint enough no one but me or Thomas would be able to tell. "*That* was about Amelia. Thomas claimed you, yes?"

I nodded, wanting to hear why Thomas was going full monkey shit over a bite that would heal in an hour or so—sooner if I had blood.

"Amelia was Thomas' progeny, a member like you are. On one of her first missions, things went sideways. She was killed by a Rogue—the woman we were meant to neutralize. Amelia was too new—she could not heal fast enough. Thomas has not made another since."

"That's great and all, but we both know Thomas didn't *make* me, and the only reason he claimed me is because Emrys had already filed the paperwork—whatever that means. He has no reason to... I'm not worth that. What Booth did was—"

"Wrong," he insisted while guiding me down the hall to a tucked away set of stairs. "There isn't another way to say what he did. Booth was only supposed to simulate a capture, not actually injure you. We discussed it before we ever started the iteration. He was never meant to bite you."

I took the stairs gently, the vibrations of the

descending steps jarring my arm. Honestly, it was all I could do not to vomit on the slick concrete.

"Then why did he?" I croaked, the pain radiating up my arm to my shoulder. Booth had done some serious tendon damage. Granted, it was nothing I couldn't heal from, but I wouldn't be winning any art contests in the near future.

"That, I don't know," he whispered, his hold more supportive and less guiding. "I'm going to pick you up now." And he did, but the result was less swoon-worthy and more nauseating. The fact that I didn't vomit all over him was a miracle.

He picked up the pace, and in no time, we were in a brightly lit room with a hospital bed and a rather harried man with glasses inspecting my injuries. He had chin-length brown hair and a hunched quality to his shoulders that made me almost believe he wasn't as big as he actually was. I could only assume this was Axel.

"She's been with us a day, Cartwright. You break her already?" Axel teased, his Southern accent thick as molasses. It wasn't exactly a Tennessee accent. Maybe Texan? He had a winsome smile I would have appreciated better had I not been bleeding out.

"Not me." Bastian set me down on the hospital bed, the paper crackling underneath my ass. "Blame Booth. He tore into her like a complete asshole. No one knows why, but rest assured, Thomas will pull it out of him. That or bash his skull in."

Axel whistled a disbelieving tune. "Booth? That teddy bear?" To me, he said, "Let's see what we're working with here. You have any regenerative abilities I should know about?"

"If you give me some blood—from a blood bag—I should be fine in an hour or so."

Axel rolled his whisky-colored eyes at me. "That stuff? Why don't you take it from the vein?" He didn't let me answer before he pressed on. "No offense, girly, but your arm is shredded. Based on blood loss alone, you've got about five more minutes of you being conscious before I gotta pump some blood into you. Now, you can drink from the blood bags, but that might be a hit to my stash and not leave some for the other members of the house that may need it. Plus..." He trailed off, and I had a feeling I did not want to know why.

But it was Bastian who answered for him, "Plus, if we are going to be partners, you need to trust that I have your back. You taking my blood helps cement that tie. Or at least that was how Thomas explained it to me."

I'd rather take no blood and heal on my own than have a tie to anyone in this house. A fact that was written all over my face if Bastian's answering expression was anything to go by.

"Axel? Give us the room?"

Axel gave me a pitying glance before he got up from his rolling stool. "Sure thing. Try not to kill each other. I just got this place back to normal after Harper's last incident."

Then Axel swept out of the room, leaving me to Bastian and his ridiculous need to feed me his blood.

Sure.

Because there was no way that could go wrong.

13

"Thomas warned me about this, you know," Bastian began, his voice pitched low, his booted feet striding close but not piercing my bubble.

I kept my gaze latched onto his feet and refused to look up. If I caught sight of his neck, of his blood pulsing in that lovely vein, I'd lose it. I wasn't hungry yet, and I wanted to keep it that way.

I cleared my throat, an action that took far too much effort and hurt for some reason. My throat was dry. Why was it so dry? "Warned you about what?"

"He said that, in time, I would want to be bitten. That the thought of you hungry or in pain would make me want to serve myself up so you didn't suffer. That it was dangerous and blissful and would likely cause you to leave us."

His feet moved closer, piercing my bubble. The heat of him washed over me, even though he was a few feet away.

I shook my head, which I instantly regretted because blood loss was a thing and I was losing a lot of it, the healing process taking far too long. Booth must have hit an artery.

"I don't want to be tied to anyone. I don't want a home. I don't want friends." It was a lie—a whole mountain of lies—but it was the truth, too. I didn't want a tie to someone who was going to leave me. I didn't want a home if I was going to lose it. I didn't want friends that would die on me.

"Too bad. Because if you think I'm going to let you leave now, you're dreaming. Now drink, you stubborn woman, or you're going to pass out."

Let me leave? He couldn't make me stay if I didn't want to. I shook my head again—a serious mistake I kept making—and a moan ripped its way up my throat. The room tilted hard, and I barely caught myself on my uninjured hand, stopping myself from falling ass over tea kettle onto the floor.

"Stubborn bloody woman," Bastian growled before he was in my bubble for real, his big body shoving itself between my legs. His giant hand threaded through my short hair, and I found my face pressed to his neck.

My senses were hit like a battering ram. Bastian's heat slammed into me, his pulse thundered in my ears, his scent filled my nose. I hadn't realized I was so cold or so hungry. I shivered—not with want or need, but because the warmth felt so good. Had I always been that cold?

Bastian's grip tightened, shaking me a little. "Drink, dammit, before I slice myself open."

His throat was right there, and I was so hungry. Instinct finally took over as my fangs lengthened and I pressed them into his neck, the gentle pop sounding in my ears as his flesh gave way.

Blood rushed into my mouth, the decadent taste warming me from the inside out. And then it wasn't just Bastian holding me to him, it was me holding him back as I reveled in the healing, the safety, the warmth. All the things I said I didn't want but craved like the touch-starved neurotic mess I was. Images came, too, but they weren't of Bastian's past or the wrongs he'd done. No, what I saw was our naked bodies tangled in sheets, his teeth nibbling at my collarbone, his body on top of mine, writhing with mine.

Bastian's hand fisted in my hair, and I swallowed, letting the hot nectar flow down my throat. Letting it heal me, letting it fill my whole body with warmth. His grip got tighter, but not pulling, the gentle pressure more of an encouragement than refusal. His scent bombarded my nose, the desire thick on the air as his other arm banded around my back and pulled me closer. His body flush with mine, I couldn't miss the thick ridge pressing against my center, his arousal calling to my own.

I swallowed again, and he answered it with a groan, the deep rumble radiating from his chest and into mine. I felt that groan all the way down to my toes and all the way up to my hair. I felt it like it was hands pressing into my flesh. And then the hand in my hair pulled, yanking my fangs from his neck before his mouth slammed down on mine.

The surprise lasted less than a second, my body overriding my brain, smacking down all my reservations with a single brush of Bastian's lips. My brain wanted to protest—hard—but my body wanted to roll in his scent, wanted to taste the inside of his mouth, wanted to see if I could make him make that delicious sound again. The remnant of his blood was still on my lips, but I did not care and neither did Bastian. His tongue swept into my mouth, a dueling dance that made me pull him tighter, hold him closer.

His scent, his heat, his touch was my whole world,

and I wanted to revel in it. Added with the images still flowing from him, it was all I could do not to make those pictures in my head a reality. Somehow my hands found themselves under his shirt, the scalding heat of his skin seeping into my palms as he gave me the most delicious of shudders, pulling another groan from his lips. Dear sweet mother of all that was holy. At that moment I would have given anything to make him make that sound again.

A loud clearing of a throat had the pair of us freezing. Well, it had *me* freezing, my hands stilling on Bastian's skin like I was hiding from a T-Rex. Bastian, however, finished the kiss, his teeth nipping at my bottom lip like he had all the time in the world. When that was done—and the shudder of need slammed into me—he gave me the most beatific of smiles. Half-naughty schoolboy, half-innocent angel, that smile did funny things to my insides. Funny things I did not want to inspect for my own sanity.

"How can I help you, Thomas?" Bastian called, his gaze not moving from mine as he examined my expression.

Thomas' tone was clipped, an irritated sort of chiding one would give a toddler. "You can start by making sure you get your wounds closed. She can't use you if you're dead."

Shit. The scent of Bastian's blood filled my nose, the wounds on his neck still seeping blood.

"Anything else? I was busy."

I had never been so happy that Bastian was enormous. His wide shoulders hid me from Thomas' stare—not that I could have looked at him anyway since Bastian's hand was still fisted in my hair.

"You remember what I told you?" Thomas asked. "About how a vampire's bite was drugging?"

Bastian's gaze did not waver, but his smile died. "Of course. But you and I both know that Sloane is not a vampire."

"If it walks like a duck," Thomas muttered. "Are you capable of being her partner, or shall I pair her with someone who will make sure her wounds are healed prior to shoving his tongue down her throat?"

"Why are you here, Thomas?" I asked, my voice squeaky like a prepubescent boy, but whatever. I'd just been caught making out with the guy who attacked me... Was that yesterday? Okay, so his censure *might* be warranted.

"I'm here to make sure you don't kill him by accident. Also, I find that I don't like the idea of you two being partners. How do I know he's going to look out for you when he's too busy staring at your ass?"

Thomas's tone was sharp enough that I ducked around Bastian's big body to stare at him.

"The not killing him part—as you can see—is not a problem. Unless you think I was draining him dry via his mouth." I shifted Bastian away from me so I could face Thomas. "And I didn't see him distracted when he was lobbing energy balls at my head or planning with Booth to jump me. I think he'll do just fine. But in the off chance he doesn't? I've survived for a year on my own with no home or a single person to look out for me. In that time? I've killed over three hundred arcaners. Wiped out entire packs of lycanthropes by myself. Taken out ghouls and vamps and mages. Alone. The question isn't if he'll watch my back, because I don't need him to. The question, Thomas, is whether or not I'll watch his."

"Bloody fucking hell. You took down the Clayborn pack?" Bastian whispered, the awe in his tone a good sign since I was still staring Thomas down.

The Clayborn pack had been a hodge-podge group of Rogue lycanthropes. It had taken three weeks, but I managed to wipe every last one of those heart-eating murderers off the map. It had been my first order of business after my first feeding, and I gleaned that the man I drank down wasn't the only one, but part of a group of raping, heart-eating, sadists with the sole, single-minded goal of growing their ranks.

"Yes, I did. By myself." My gaze did not waver from Thomas. His entire body was still. I didn't even think he was breathing.

"How?" Thomas growled, the single word like a whip cracking.

"When I woke up on my grave, I didn't know what I was. I was going to the police to see if they could help and cut through an alley. A vampire named Jacob attacked me and I killed him. After that, I didn't go to the police and I didn't feed again, horrified at what I was. I didn't eat for a week. I figured I could starve myself to death because the sun didn't hurt and holy water wouldn't work, and everything else I tried, I healed from. A lycanthrope broke into a warehouse near the place I was holed up—he raped and murdered a woman. I smelled the blood, and I couldn't stop myself. Reading his soul, I found out he wasn't alone, so I hunted them down one by one."

Thomas approached, his movements too fast to track, and he was in my face, barely an inch from my nose. "No. How did you kill them? How did you find them? How did you make them suffer? I want the details."

Stupidly, Bastian put a hand on Thomas' shoulder. Thomas swatted it off so hard I heard the bones crack. Bastian howled in rage and a bit of agony, but Thomas did not move again, his pale-green stare like shards of glass piercing me to the table.

"Tell me," he ordered, his voice like silk.

I felt the pressure of him using his magic on me. Some called it compulsion, some called it the charm, some called it hypnosis. It was all pretty words for the magic vampires had that took a person's will away.

"Not if you're going to try and use that stupid fucking magic on me," I growled, shoving off the table and pushing him away. "You calm down, and maybe I'll tell you. But it was three weeks of bloody work, and the things I saw were..." I shook my head and gave him my back, turning to Bastian to assess his injuries.

Rather than the broken hand I thought he'd have, he sported a few dislocated fingers instead. Growling, he yanked each back in place like the action wouldn't cause anyone else to puke their guts out on the tile floor.

"I owe you a debt," Thomas whispered, his voice clogged with an emotion I couldn't name. "I will owe you forever. That pack took someone very precious away from me. Someone I will miss for the rest of my exceedingly long life. If there is anything you need of me, I will provide."

Then I felt the displacement of the air and the faintest of whooshing sounds and Thomas was gone.

Bastian flexed his fingers, the motion slow as he

134 | ANNIE ANDERSON

tested his healing hand. The blood on his neck had clot-
ted, but the wounds looked angry and painful. Still, he
appeared as if the pain did not register.

"The Clayborn pack was the one we were hunting
when Amelia died. After her death, they vanished,
hopping from city to city, disappearing like smoke as
soon as we got close. Thomas has been searching for
them for seventy-five years, and you took them out in
three weeks."

I didn't know how I felt about that. I wasn't doing
anything special other than hunting bad men. At the
time it felt like if I was going to be a monster, I might as
well kill worse monsters.

"Thomas isn't the only person who owes you, you
know."

I rolled my eyes, exasperated at the whole conversation. I didn't want people to owe me anything.

"Awesome. Who else owes me?"

"I do."

14

My gaze whipped back to Bastian, but he didn't meet my eyes. Shame colored every line of his face as his jaw tightened.

"Why do you owe me?" I was unable to hold the question in any longer.

He lifted his head, spearing me with his sharp gaze. "I just do."

And then he was gone. Without another word, without any explanation, he just left the room, abandoning me to get back on my own.

Some partner he was.

For the first—well, second, but semantics and all that —time since I'd been bitten, I looked down at my injured arm. While still a bloody mess, the skin had knitted back together, the flesh seemingly healed. With nothing else to do besides fret over what the fuck was going on with Bastian, I hopped off the examination table and went to the sink.

I was still reeling from his abrupt departure and Thomas losing it over the Clayborn pack, and all the rest of the changes my life had undergone in the last day and a half. And why did Booth bite me? And why was Simon so freaked?

Well, that one might have made a little more sense now that I'd made out with his brother. As I washed the blood off my hand, I thought about Bastian's lips on mine, his hand in my hair, the scent of him...

Stop it. This is exactly the wrong thing to be thinking about.

As much as my conscience was yelling at me, I couldn't stop the shiver that worked its way through me at the thought of Bastian's hand in my hair, the way he pulled me off his neck and kissed me, the heat of his skin under my palms.

Fuck.

Was it just because he was willing? Was it the blood? Was it the thoughts and images that bombarded me when I read his soul? I could almost feel them again, the memory so vivid. Was that what he wanted? Or because he knew what I was, was that all he was willing to show me?

A cold bucket of libido-killing ice washed over me.

He knew I was a soul reader, he could be guarding his mind against me, only showing me those things to hide what was really in his heart. I couldn't say why that felt like a betrayal, why it felt like I'd been stabbed in the chest at the thought, but it did.

But didn't he deserve to hide from me? Wasn't that his right? I was offered his blood, not his soul. I was offered sustenance, not his secrets. Still, the thought of him hiding on purpose hurt me in ways I was not prepared for.

Then I groaned out loud, the sound echoing off the sterile walls and metal cabinets filled with medical supplies. Simon was so right, and I was an idiot for thinking he had no idea. Bastian and I should most definitely not enter into a relationship.

It was going to be blood bags or nothing from here on out.

After I'd washed off all the blood and cleaned up the sink with cleanser and some paper towels, Axel strode back in the room. Now that I wasn't damn near bleeding to death, I took the time to assess him fully.

When he wasn't hunched on an examination stool, he was quite tall, his broad shoulders held back in a sauntering sort of way that spoke of an easy-going attitude and general jovial nature. His chin-length hair had been brushed back from his face, a streak of gray threaded through it that I hadn't noticed before. He was dressed in jeans, a western-style long-sleeved shirt with snap buttons, and cowboy boots. I'd lived in the South my whole life, and no one in the history of ever, pulled off that look better than Axel.

"Well, I see my med bay is still intact, and you're healed up nice." He picked up my arm to examine the former wound, his hands like ice. "Not even a scar. I'm impressed. Thomas is the only one who can heal that fast from blood consumption, and he's *old*. You're a young thing. How do you heal faster than Thomas?"

"Just lucky, I guess," I muttered before pulling my arm out of his loose hold and blurting the thing that had been on my mind since Bastian left the room. "I need you to get more blood bags." Sighing, I closed my eyes and started again. "I fed from Bastian this time, but I would really appreciate it if you would increase your stock of blood. While it may taste like swill, and it might not work as well—"

"You'd rather drink hot garbage than fall into bed with the man?" Axel cut me off, his assessment blunt but accurate. He tapped his nose. "It smells like mind-numbing lust in this room."

"Essentially." It was a major slight to Bastian, but dammit, I was not risking everything I was when I didn't have that much left to give. I needed to give to me first, for fuck's sake.

Axel's smile bloomed over his face, his teeth impossibly straight and white. It was a movie-star smile which took his already-blinding hotness to stratospheric levels. Good god, were all arcaners this hot? I didn't remember the Rogues I'd killed being this pleasing to look at.

"Well, I would suggest getting another partner, but there aren't many of us you could feed from. Me and Thomas are out. Undead blood won't nourish you the same way live blood will. Dahlia's anemic, Harper can't stand to be touched, and Simon…"

"Is a no-go because Bastian will go full monkey shit, and I wouldn't touch Booth with a ten-foot pole. So that leaves the bags."

Axel pursed his lips as he folded himself into a chair. "I'll put in an order. You got a preference in type?"

"Not that I know of. And thank you for understanding. I've been alone for a while now, and I kind of like it here. I'd rather not fuck it all up in the first week, you know?"

He nodded sagely, like I was actually talking sense, which made me feel like I was doing the right thing. No more feedings—not from Bastian.

Axel tapped his bottom lip with his index finger. "Emrys said you were a soul reader—not that I've ever seen one of ya'll in the wild. You're supposed to be able to read the blood of a person, right?"

Instantly, I was wary. "Yeah?"

He seemed to pick up on my trepidation because he hunched his shoulders, resting his elbows on his knees. I wondered if he was used to doing that—making himself appear smaller to make people more comfortable. "Emrys said she wanted to wait, but I have a victim I can't identify, and I could really use your help."

"Victim?" I took a small step backward. "What do you mean by victim?"

Axel sighed, running a hand through his hair. "Booth and I just got back from a job. We were hunting down a Rogue that's been responsible for some maulings, but we haven't been able to catch the bastard. Most of the victims have survived, but this one didn't. She's tore up pretty bad, and we can't identify her."

I winced, thinking about drinking blood from a dead body. "And you want my help."

On the one hand, it sounded disgusting as fuck. On the other, I was offered a place here. I couldn't exactly turn my nose up at the first chance to use my abilities in a non-murdery way. I must not have been very good at wiping the *ewwww* off my face because Axel started chuckling.

"You won't have to bite her," he reassured me. "I'll

draw some blood with a syringe. You won't even have to look at her if you don't want to."

Swallowing down a fair bit of bile, I nodded. "Okay, sure," I croaked. "If I can help, I will."

"That's the spirit. How much blood do you need?"

I thought back to all the times I'd read a person right before I killed them. Usually, it only took a single pull before I knew every single wrong they'd ever done, every sin etched into their soul.

"A swallow?" I shrugged. "I usually know all I need to after the first pull, so like an ounce?"

Axel got up from his stool and snagged a syringe before heading back to a door that looked like a walk-in freezer. Quick as a whip, he was back with a full syringe which he emptied into a plastic cup.

"Bottom's up," he said, grinning at what was likely my sourpuss face.

Dead blood. I shuddered, and then hauled up my big girl panties, downing the viscous liquid like a shot.

Instantly, I realized I had just done a very bad thing. This wasn't like the flashes of images I got from Jacob or the ephemeral smoke of Bastian's inner thoughts. This was a visceral bombardment of every sense, every thought, every sin. This was hell itself.

Only it wasn't mine.

Time seemed to go backward from the point of her

death, her last gasp of breath was in my lungs, the bitter regret racing through her veins. The frantic pawing at her attacker, even though they had already delivered her death knell. The icy-blue glint of the big cat right before it lunged, and on and on it went.

And it wasn't until I saw my face, my parents' faces, did I realize who it was. Whose blood I'd drank, whose life had been stolen.

Aunt Julie.

I wanted to pull out of the read, but I was stuck, the images coming faster, the pain in them as real as if I were there.

But more, it was the visions she saw, the deaths she'd predicted. Including her own. She wasn't human, had never been.

Aunt Julie.

My mother's best friend, my surrogate parent, my friend, my family. The last family I had. I'd considered going to her after I'd woken up, but after Jacob, I'd figured that it would be better if I didn't. Better if I just stayed dead.

And now she was dead.

The visions spun faster, the pain ripping me apart piece by piece. Everything I'd thought was true, everything I'd believed. It was all gone.

A hand on my shoulder caused a tortured moan to

leak out of my throat. A bucket was forced in my hands, and as if on cue, I vomited into it. The pain and rage and sorrow coming up with the blood.

I had to get it out, I couldn't let it stay in me.

Aunt Julie.

A warm hand was on my back, but I shrugged it off before tossing more cookies into the bucket until I was shaking and spent, my gut aching with loss and the agony of the knowledge that my last bit of family was gone from this world. My brain just couldn't hang on to anything but the image of the big cat ripping through her flesh, the burning, shredding, torture of claws rending her muscle and skin and bone.

I heaved again, but nothing came up. Tears poured down my face, the sound of my sobs echoing through the sparse med bay like some sort of tortured animal.

"Here, drink this," someone said, handing me a bottle of water. Someone else put a cold washcloth on my neck, and someone else took the bucket away from my hands.

Someone was crying, great, bitter sobs of pain, the sound like the worst kind of torture. It didn't take too long to realize that those sobs—the ones that hurt my heart to hear—were coming from me.

"Sloane, sweetie, I need you to tell me what you saw," Axel urged, his tone soft as silk. "And I'm gonna need you to calm down while you do it. I don't wanna pump you full of benzos, but I will."

An image flashed—one I'd seen before and would never forget—the big cat, its blue eyes flashing as its claws extended. Its white fur matted with blood as it struck again and again, rending flesh and bone, cutting into her like she was tissue paper.

Then a new image—full of fire and pain and my twisted face.

And despite Axel's warnings, despite the comforting hands and well wishes, I started screaming. I didn't stop until Axel pumped me full of drugs, but even then, I dreamed of Julie's torture, of her memories, of her visions.

Those stayed, and they would cling to me.

Forever.

15

I shuddered, even though it was warm in my house, the heater working double-time to combat the coming winter chill. But visions brought their own form of cold, and no matter the weather, no matter what I did, I would always feel the finger of doom on my back.

One was coming, I knew as much, but I never knew when. I snuggled under my blanket, setting my book down before I lost my page. Visions came every day, but a good book series? Those were rare, and oracle or not, I didn't want the ending spoiled if I accidentally lost my place.

As soon as I put the book down, a premonition slammed into me of a giant home set away from the city. It had a gray façade with elegant architecture and a midnight-blue door. Men were surrounding it, guns in their hands and spells on their belt, their *tactical gear loaded down with magical weapons and enough potions to stop a rhinoceros—or an ancient vampire.*

They blasted their way through a ward, their numbers too great for the magic to hold, spells firing right along with the guns. They had a singular focus, and it was not one of capture.

This was a kill order.

This was the end of the Night Watch.

A hand on mine had me rocketing out of my drugged sleep, scrambling out of the heavy covers as I practically climbed up the headboard.

"Whoa, girly. No need to climb the walls," a voice called, and I had to blink—hard—to focus on her face. *Harper.*

I wouldn't say I was exactly relaxed after my waking scare, but I did remove myself from the giant headboard. I didn't get any closer to her, though, keeping the large bed between us as she moved to the stool at the drafting table.

"They sent me in here to see if I could help." She held up her hand, wiggling her fingers. "I can affect emotions, not just feel them. I don't use it very often because it bypasses mental warding, but you'd been stuck in whatever hell loop you were in for about half a day. Emrys wanted to see if I could pull you out." She wiped at her eyes with the back of her hand, smearing her carefully applied eye makeup.

She was crying. Why was she crying? Why was she here? What happened to me?

"I'm going on facial cues here since it seems talking is out of your wheelhouse for the time being, but I'm thinking you're confused? Yeah, we all are, kid. Best guess—and this is what I heard from Axel and Thomas —you tried to help him identify a body and it went sideways. Well, more than sideways."

Aunt Julie.

Harper frowned, leaning closer. "Who's Aunt Julie?"

Had I said that out loud? "The body—the woman in the cold room," I croaked. "She is—*was*—my mother's best friend. Juliet Hearst. Aunt Julie."

I didn't tell Harper all I'd seen—all I'd felt. There was no way to put it into words. No way to quantify and measure the agony of her death, the cold ache of her visions, the bitter pill that my entire life had been one lie after the other.

My parents weren't human and had never been. Neither had Aunt Julie. They spelled me, hid me away, lied to me. Because of what I was?

I pressed my eyes closed, the images of her soul hitting me like physical blows. No other reading had ever felt like this. Was it because she was already dead? Was it because she was my family? Was it because despite her faults, Julie had been good?

And she was gone—just like my parents.

A gentle thump radiated through the mattress as Isis jumped onto my bed, the skeleton cat padding her way over the covers to me. Dutifully, I eased from my crouch, allowing the bone kitty to curl up on my lap. Could she sense that I was about to lose it? Or had Simon sent her?

"I've never met a soul reader, so I don't know if knowing someone beforehand makes the reading worse. Given your reaction—and the manner of her death—I'd say reading from the dead is not the best idea."

I gave her a "no shit" look. *Way to state the obvious, Harper.* "I want to see her."

Harper's answering expression was startled and horrified. "Why?"

"Because she is the last of my family, and now she's dead. Because I never got to see my parents or say goodbye to them. I just woke up in a fucking cemetery looking at their goddamn graves. Because I fucking want to, that's why."

She raised her hands in surrender. "Okay, okay. No need to bite my head off. It's just..." She trailed off, wiping another ribbon of tears from her cheek. "I felt what you were feeling, and it was some of the worst pain I've ever..." She shook her head, unable to go on. "I can't do that again, Sloane. I can't pull you out again. I'll go crazy."

Isis began to purr at me, and I absently started scratching under her chin.

"I wouldn't want you to. No one ever needs to feel like that if they don't have to. But I need to see her. If just to say goodbye."

"I'll ask, but I'm telling you, Emrys might lock you up in a padded cell if you lose it again. That was... that was..." She trailed off, shaking her head. With a rueful twist to her lips, she shoved off the stool and strode out of the room.

I wanted to tell her sorry, wanted to take back whatever pain I'd shoveled her way, but the scars were too new and the pain too fresh, so I said nothing. Instead I cooed at a skeleton cat, and prayed my hold on sanity lasted just a bit longer.

Not five minutes later, a quiet rap on my door heralded a visit from Emrys. No longer in a white suit, she seemed almost normal in an eggplant tunic and leggings. Her feet were bare, and it was then that I noticed how short she was. When I first met her, she seemed larger than life and twice as big. Now that everything I had left had been ripped apart, everything seemed smaller. Everything seemed colorless and cruel.

Everything hurt.

"It's good to see you awake, Sloane," she said, sitting on the stool Harper vacated. "I have to say, if this is how it goes after every read, I'm going to have to rethink your purpose here. After what we all saw, my girl, I could not willfully put you through that again—no matter what the gain may be."

Alarm filled me before I stomped it down, letting the pain of losing another home glance off me. I mean, why wouldn't she kick me out? I was no more useful than tits on a bull if I couldn't read people.

I ran my hands over the lush bedding before cuddling Isis closer. Her purr was a balm I would miss greatly. I'd miss the roof over my head and the people. How much would going back to the streets hurt? Would it be worse now since I'd been in such a lavish place? Or since I was here for such a short time, would the memory fade?

A single hot tear scorched down my cheek before I hastily wiped it away.

"Oh, no, Sloane. I'm not suggesting you'd be kicked out," Emrys blurted, moving from the stool to the side of the bed. "I only meant that you'd have a different job. Given the state of Booth's jaw, I figure you could be our muscle. Thomas so rarely goes out in the field anymore."

I gave her a sad imitation of a smile, which was about all I could muster.

"Harper tells me you want to see the body. That the woman was your family?"

A burning sort of ache started in my chest, the flames growing with every breath. All I could do was nod. "Juliet Hearst. She was my mother's best friend. She—she was an oracle."

Not that I knew that information when she was alive. Not that I understood what her last vision meant or why it came about, or if it was true.

This was the end of the Night Watch.

Was it because I was here?

Were people coming for me?

Or had her vision already come and gone with nothing to show for it. I saw in her memories that they often did—a person's decision changed, altering their course and making the vision moot. Was this one of those times?

Or was it the reason she was killed?

Was *I* the reason she was killed?

I was so busy with the thoughts swirling in my head, that I almost missed it when Emrys' face went pale as a sheet.

"An oracle, you said?" Emrys abruptly stood, shoving to her feet like she had a purpose. "You don't plan on reading her again, correct?"

I didn't have a plan for anything, but the more I

thought about it, the more I realized I would need to read her again, need to see if I could glean more from Julie's last moments. She was murdered and I wanted to know by who.

"Sloane?" Emrys prompted, reminding me that I hadn't answered her.

"I don't know. She was murdered by a big white cat, but something about it was familiar and I don't know why. I owe it to her to find out who killed her. Maybe…"

Maybe if I found that person, I'd find out what happened to my parents.

"Maybe we'll get some answers," I finished, heading for the door.

I could do this.

I could.

Right?

Emrys was hot on my heels as I forced myself down the stairs. "May I ask, has it ever been like that for you before?"

I shuddered, hard, and shook my head, not stopping, not slowing down. If I hesitated for a millisecond, I wouldn't have the courage to go back. "Never. I couldn't say if it was because I knew her or because she was already dead when I drank her blood. Truth be told, I'm not all too geared up to find out."

You know why. It was because of what she saw. What she knew. Someone wanted her silent.

That thought came blazing through my brain right as I reached the staircase to the basement. If I read her again, would someone want *me* silent? Could I trust the people in this house? Axel and Booth were chasing a shifter, but how easily could that be a ruse?

How easily could the people in this house lie to my face?

I forced myself to walk down the steps to the med bay, the sterile room more populated than I'd hoped for. Axel was perched on his stool, facing off a harried-looking Bastian and a fanged-out Thomas.

Goodie. Just what I need on this fine morning. An audience.

"Sloane," Thomas breathed as he approached, his sclera returning to white as his fangs receded back into the periodontal pockets that housed them when he wasn't being emotional. He looked like he wanted to hug me, but settled on a reassuring squeeze to my shoulder. "You sure gave us a scare, kid."

I probably should have said something pithy to bolster his spirits, but I just didn't have it in me. My subdued attitude went over like a lead balloon, leaving the men shifting their feet as they struggled to look at me.

They knew something. I could feel the lie on the air

as if one had been spoken aloud. They knew something and they were hiding it.

"I want to see her," I murmured, my voice barely a whisper.

They could have their secrets. I'd figure this out by myself, like I always had.

And no one was going to stop me.

16

The three men shifted on their feet again, and it was all I could do not to growl at them.

"I don't think that is a smart plan, Sloane," Bastian advised.

Had I not just been given the worst blow imaginable, I would have marveled at the fact that this was the first time he'd actually called me by name. As it stood, I was just irritated he was in my way.

"You said everyone here has a sad story, right?" I began, my eyebrows raised, my face demanding an answer. He gave me a sharp bob of his head. "How many of you were able to say goodbye to those you lost? Bury them? Shed a tear for their passing? And how many of you woke up to everyone and everything you ever knew gone just like that?" I snapped my fingers right in his face, the loud crack making him flinch. "How many of you had to live through a beloved's death? Felt every tear of their skin, every break in their bones, every feeble fluttering beat of their heart as it withered and died?"

I looked around the room, at their stricken faces. "None? No takers, then?" I speared Bastian with my gaze. "Then how about you stop with the bullshit advice for a problem you've never had and show me her fucking body."

Yes, my words were cruel. Yes, I could have gone about that a little better. But being treated like a feeble little lady in the middle of this shit wasn't going to help me. Finding the fucker who killed Julie was going to help. Finding out what happened to my parents was going to help.

Coddling was just going to drag me down into a pit of despair, and I couldn't let that happen.

Because if I fell in, I wouldn't be able to get back out.

Axel stepped to the side, his hands raised in surrender. "Okay, kid, but it took three times the recommended dosage for a shifter to put you down when you lost it. Don't make me do it to you again."

I followed him as he walked to the large door that had to be a commercial-grade refrigerator and opened it. The room was far larger than I'd expected, maybe ten by twelve feet. It had a wall full of empty slabs, and a lone

one in the middle. A black body bag lay on the silver steel table, and despite my earlier bravado, I shivered.

"Now, I know you wanna see her, Sloane, but she ain't pretty." he advised, a gentle concern laced through his words. "The shifter tore into her something awful, and I want you to brace yourself for what you're about to see."

Axel carefully unzipped the bag, the tines parting one by one in the slowest agony ever. I'd seen my fair share of dead bodies. Hell, I'd made more than my fair share, but I never ripped them up. Save for eight puncture wounds—and the occasional throat rippage—my dead appeared mostly as they had in life. Julie was *not* as carefully killed. I knew that much from feeling her death, watching from her eyes as she was slashed and broken.

But seeing it from the outside was worse somehow.

Her face was a bloody mess, half of her jaw missing, her eyes gone from their sockets. Her chest was cut wide, her abdomen empty, the edges of the cavity jagged like...

"Did the shifter... eat her?" I asked, horrified at what I was seeing.

Axel gave me a slow nod. "I think so. He's acting like a wild animal and going for the soft parts. I've never seen a shifter do that—not that wasn't feral and stuck in his animal, anyway. You said it was a big cat?"

I nodded, staring at the lone bit of unmarred skin on Julie's forehead right above her left eyebrow. I bent, pressing a kiss to that bit of skin, her flesh cold against my lips.

Goodbye, Julie. I hope wherever you are, you're at peace.

Rising up from my farewell, I sniffed. Not from tears, those, I feared were gone forever. No, I wanted to know her scent, or rather *his* scent. "The scent patterns in this room are too varied. Do you have any of her clothing?"

Rather than look at Axel, I snagged the zipper and hauled it up, covering her destroyed body as the rest of me went cold. The frost of her skin seeped into my bones, turning me to stone even as I mentally finished my goodbyes.

I didn't need emotions or a conscience. I had no use for pleasantries or niceties. It was time to work.

Hadn't I been doing that for the last year? Hadn't killing Jacob led to the Clayborn pack? Hadn't they led to a nest of ghouls picking off elderly patients of a retirement home? Hadn't those ghouls led to a tiny pocket of Rogue witches stealing children? And on and on and on until I was cleaning up the streets every single day for a year?

I knew how to hunt an enemy, knew how to stalk my prey until they were cornered with no way out.

I couldn't die—*trust me, I'd tried*—so I had nothing

but time on my hands. And now with Julie gone, I really did have nothing to lose.

"Yeah, I have them, but I smelled them and all I got was Booth's scent off of them." He strode out of the walk-in fridge to snag a large plastic bag off his desk. "But he's the one who found her and carried her out. You could see if your nose is better than mine."

He handed me the bag, and I opened the zippered top. At first all I got was the scent of decaying blood, bile, loose bowels, and urine and had to shove down a gag. Then the bouquet of other scents wafted out. The earthy tang of shifter—Booth specifically. He was all over her clothes almost masking Julie's light floral signature.

Well, that was a bust.

I zippered the pouch shut and handed it back. "I'll need to see her home then. I'm not getting anything but Julie and Booth."

Axel looked worried. "I don't—"

"No offense, Axel, but I really don't give a shit what *you don't*. I've done nothing but hunt arcaners for the last year. It's what I'm good at. Why don't you just save your misgivings until I'm writhing in pain on your floor. Cool?"

"What about us?" Thomas broke in. "You give a shit what we think, or are you going off half-cocked no matter what we say?"

Bastian, Thomas, and Emrys stood off to the side in a little huddle, but I didn't find censure in anyone's expression. A little pain, a little empathy, a little pity, but no censure.

I pinched the bridge of my nose praying for strength. "I give a shit what you have to say if you're not standing in my way. You going to stop me, Thomas?"

Bastian stepped closer to me, moving in front of Thomas—either to protect me or Thomas, I couldn't figure out which—his face awash in an emotion I couldn't identify. "No one is going to stop you from hunting this bastard down. But we need to do this smart, and forego getting the people around us killed in the name of vengeance. Can you do that, or would you like to be locked down until the end of time?"

Protecting Thomas from me, then.

I pretended to ponder his question. "I don't know. Let me think." I tapped my lip with my index finger. "I'll take door number one, thanks. Any other manly assertions you'd like to make? Those scent patterns aren't going to stay there forever, and I've already lost too much time."

Emrys sighed like I was trying the very last bit of her patience. "I can't believe I'm saying this, but if you're going out into the field, you'll need gear. Thomas will get you outfitted. Meet up at the front door in thirty minutes."

"Are you serious?" Bastian protested. "She's one slippery step away from full-blown feral and you want her out in the field? No offense, but you made it my mission to keep her from killing arcaners and at the first turn you're just giving her what she wants? Am I the only one who sees this?"

Emrys didn't bother sparing Bastian a glance. Instead, she met and held my gaze, an understanding in them that I felt on a visceral level. She gave me the slightest of nods, a gentle bow of her head that spoke of her own loss, her own pain. She recognized it in me. She knew my pain as acutely as I did.

"Mr. Cartwright, do you think I'm a fool?" Emrys raised her eyebrows in challenge. Bastian's deer-in-the-headlights expression was answer enough because she continued, "I thought not. There is a very good reason why I will be accompanying you on this excursion. Rest assured that the responsibility of Sloane's compliance will rest on someone else's shoulders."

Thomas skirted around Bastian and Emrys' tableau and wrapped an arm around my shoulders. "Come on, kid. Let's get you outfitted."

. . .

It turned out that Clem of all people was actually in charge of the gear, weapons, and protective clothing that the Night Watch used on a daily basis.

"I don't sleep, so I need to keep busy," Clem explained as her ghostly pale fingers moved like hummingbird wings on a pair of leather pants, the hand stitching a thing of beauty. "As a girl who used to say I'd sleep when I was dead, it's a mighty big adjustment."

Clem was a Southern woman through and through— even though the body she was inhabiting was from California. She told me that little tidbit sotto voce like I'd spill her secrets to the Southern Police or something. But other than the fact that she was a certified chatterbox and well, *dead*, I had no issues with the woman.

She tied off her last stitch and then shook out the garment with a flourish. "I know you had those leather pants, but they just weren't for you, dear. This will protect you better, and Dahlia spelled the leather. Now it will repel killing spells, protect you from poisons, and it's practically bulletproof. I know, I know. Like Thomas, you'll heal from just about anything, but injuries hurt and slow you down."

I accepted the garment. It was a mix of leather and a thick flexible material strategically placed for ease of movement. The leather bits were thick and yet buttery soft. She also handed me a belt with thigh holsters attached.

"Get dressed." Clem pointed to a giant Japanese screen. Apparently, she meant right here, right now. "I'll get your weapons."

Clem might be cute as a button—a very dead button —but she wasn't someone I wanted to cross, so I followed her instruction and got to it. "Weapons?"

"You think I'm going to let you go out into the wild with nothing?" She clucked her tongue at me like I was simple. "Mama Clem has got you covered."

Typically, I would just take whatever weapons my opponents had and use the guns or knives or swords against them. I was decent with a gun, swords were not my forte, and knives were just fun. I thought about this as I slid into the suit Clem had put the finishing touches on. Other than pajamas, it was probably one of the more comfortable things I'd ever worn. It seemed made for me, which made me want to slap myself upside the head because *it was*. I buckled the front closure that secured my meager chest, the material thicker there for added protection.

A pair of low-heeled boots flew over the top of the screen, and I barely caught them before they hit me in the head.

"You coming?" Dahlia called impatiently, and I hurried to zip the boots so as to not keep her waiting.

"Yeah, yeah," I muttered, skirting around the screen and back to Clem who held out a pistol and a weird-handled *thing*. "What is that?"

The top looked like a geometric loop guard for a sword, but there was no metal tine—AKA, the actual sword part—attached.

"Ah." Dahlia grinned. "This is my brilliance, *thankyouverymuch*. I mixed mage and witch magic to make this baby. Hold it in your hand and speak the incantation, *uitta mortis*."

Reluctantly, I did as told—the weight of the handle heavy in my hand for being mostly nothing.

But when I spoke the incantation, the weight shifted, concentrating less on the handle, and flowing out in a ribbon of electric-blue light. It pooled on the ground, waiting for me to flick out the deadly energy.

And then my rusty Latin supplied the translation.

Ribbon of Death.

17

"This is a whip," I said stupidly, stating the fucking obvious. But what was this, *Temple of Doom*? Did I turn into *Indiana Jones* overnight?

Dahlia rolled her eyes at me as she put a hand on her slim hip. "Duh. Okay, so I know that whips are out of style, but it offers a way to strike your opponents from far away, and it's ridiculously cool. Sure, guns and swords are awesome, but you have a magic whip. I mean, that's original."

I raised my eyebrows at her, gently flicking the whip to get a feel for it. I had to admit, it was cool as fuck, and even if it wasn't original, it was at the very least retro. "I'm not mad at it."

"Good, because you have no other choice." Dahlia

166 | ANNIE ANDERSON

stuck her tongue out at me. "I made it for you, so no one else can use it. You're welcome."

"Thank you," I replied dutifully. "Thank you both."

"Good. Say the incantation again to get it to contract."

I obeyed, watching as the ribbon of light retracted into the handle before holstering it.

"Now that that's done, it's time to go. Clem, give her some ammo for that Glock and let's get moving."

Clem passed over four magazines, and I shoved them in the specialty-made loops in my belt, checked the mag on the Glock and chambered a round, shoving it in the holster and securing the strap. Glocks didn't have a safety, but the triggers weren't loose, and the strap added protection. If I were going out into the world, I'd need it, and arcaners moved too fast not to have a round in the chamber.

Living in the South all my life, I was comfortable with handguns. I'd shot my first .22 at seven years old. They were tried and true just like climbing mountains, pitching tents, and skinning rabbits. My parents—for all their secrets and faults—taught me how to survive. Taught me how to live in the wild, how to make shelter, how to shoot and prep game.

I wondered what my last year would have been like if I'd actually utilized their teachings and went to the hills instead of the city. Would I be here right now? Or would I be like Julie, torn apart and wishing for another path?

After my weapons check, I followed Dahlia to the front door, the midnight color causing a cold finger of dread to trace down my spine.

"Everyone ready?" Emrys asked, breaking my stare on the doomed door.

I looked around at our group. Bastian, Thomas, Emrys, and Axel joined Dahlia and I at the meeting location. Harper approached, handing each of us a comms device. The tiny black thing was no bigger than a button and was meant to fit in our ear. According to Harper, it used bone conduction and was supposed to be the latest thing in communications gear.

"Do not forget that I can hear everything you say. Thomas ended up on an interlude after some nasty wounds and forgot to take comms off." Harper shuddered like she was reliving the memory. "There are some things you can't unknow or unhear."

Thomas had the good sense to blush—a feat I didn't think possible on his undead skin. "I've apologized a thousand times for that already. How was I supposed to know she was going to be a screamer?" He sighed, pinching his brow. "Please quit using that story as a cautionary tale."

Harper gave him a look that could fry metal. "When I

get the sound of you fucking a blood junkie out of my brain, I'll quit mentioning it to any and everyone I give comms to. Until then, you're shit out of luck."

I wanted to laugh for the first time since I'd woken up, and the nearly silent giggle slipped past my lips against my better judgment. Quickly, it turned into an actual laugh until I was practically rolling on the floor. I imagined Harper's face as she scrambled to turn off the comms, having it turn into a slapstick because she was flustered, and the volume turn louder instead of off. I could practically see it in my head.

"Oh, man. I needed that. Never change, Harper. Never."

Harper stuck her tongue out at me, and I blew her a kiss.

Emrys cleared her throat. "We'll all be in the same transport, but here are your teams: Axel and Dahlia, Thomas and I, and Bastian and Sloane. Harper, Simon, and Booth are staying here. Comms check?" We all put the devices in our ears to perform the check, getting a nod from Harper. "Fabulous. Let's roll out."

We followed Emrys as she led us past the front door, down the hall, and to a garage. Among the many cars was a black SUV with dark tinted windows and a ram guard on the front grill. It appeared weighted down as if it were armored, and I realized pretty quickly that it must be. I piled in the third-row seat, Bastian following me, and then we were off.

The drive to my hometown of Whispering Pines was shorter than I thought it would be. For some reason, in my head I pictured the Night Watch house being farther away than just on the rural outskirts of Ascension. We skirted around the city to get to my little suburb, passing the college I'd gone to on the way to Julie's house. On the other side of town was my childhood home, and I stared in that direction, even though I wouldn't be able to see it. The burned-out wreck called to me even now.

I swallowed, hard, and tried to get my head back in the game. My parents were long dead, but Julie wasn't. Her house had to have some clues. There had to be something there. A scent pattern that was missed, blood somewhere that wasn't Julie's, something. Axel navigated the streets like he'd lived here his whole life, cutting into alleys to avoid being seen.

Evidently there were video cameras on everyone's front porch nowadays, but oh, so rarely did people bother putting a camera on the back entrance, making it vulnerable to attack. Or at least in our case, it made it so some shmuck with a twenty-dollar camera couldn't record something he shouldn't.

Unerringly, Axel found the alley driveway of Julie's

former home, the garbage cans set on the curb like it was a normal Thursday night. Did her neighbors know that their friend was dead? Did they hear her being ripped apart? Or were the houses too far apart, the sound too faint for their elderly human ears?

We piled out of the SUV, and I got a good look at the house I'd spent a good portion of my childhood in. A flash of memory superimposed itself on the dark yard. Mom and Aunt Julie cackling at the kitchen table while I drew in the living room. Dad barbecuing on her deck while I played with Otis in the backyard.

But then Axel opened the back sliding glass door, and the memory was shattered. Reluctantly—even though it was my fucking idea—I entered Julie's home. The dining chairs were upended, the table on its side. Blood drips and smears were all over the kitchen. The open-concept space led directly to the living room, the couch cushions a tattered mess of fluff and blood.

I knew from her memories that Julie had tried to fend off her attacker, catching him with the fireplace poker as she fled upstairs. But Julie had been no match for the shifter, and she'd only made it to the top landing before she'd been caught.

Everything I was seeing supported Julie's memories. The blood trails, the scent of her fear clinging to them as if the urgency were still there, a warning to all who entered that the danger had not passed.

Emrys and Dahlia were searching for personal effects to use in case my nose wasn't up to snuff. Axel and Thomas were playing lookout, stationed at the front and back entrances to make sure no one returned to see if there were more victims to be had. And Bastian and I were tasked with identifying scent patterns and looking for clues.

I had a feeling everyone was humoring me. Axel and Booth had been at this a lot longer than I had, and likely had already swept for clues. This excursion was more like they were coddling a toddler who'd thrown the mother of all hissy fits rather than a legitimate mission.

Not that I could blame them. Still, I followed Julie's blood trail from the kitchen where she'd first been struck to the living room where she grabbed the poker. The shifter had scored another hit on the couch, the slashing claw marks telling the tale as they mingled with Julie's blood. She vaulted over the couch, knocking over the console table and lamp, which shattered and cut her arm open. Then she'd hidden behind the couch, readying her weapon.

When the cat pounced, it got a shoulder full of wrought-iron poker. I saw it clearly in her memories, the poker piercing his flesh and fur, the spill of blood splashing on the hardwood floor. But where there should be a puddle, there was none. In fact, it was the one part of this whole space that was free of debris, of blood, of glass.

It smelled of cleanser.

"Well, fuck," I muttered, damn near stomping my feet.

"What?" Bastian's gaze scanned the room, his nose not telling him the same story mine was telling me.

"Julie stabbed her attacker with a poker. You see this spot?" I pointed at the circle of clean space. "The fucker used cleanser to clean up his own blood. And from the looks of it, he took the damn poker with him."

"Fuck."

I nodded in commiseration. I wasn't getting anything but Julie and Booth in here with the teensiest bit of Axel thrown in.

"Are there any droplets away from the scene? He couldn't have cleaned them all, right?"

We followed Julie's blood trail upstairs, but all I smelled was her. This was a bust—just like everyone probably thought it would be.

Rather than pause at the giant pool of blood on the landing, I turned left, walking into Julie's bedroom. Her bed was unmade, the clothes she'd worn the day before draped over the bench at the end of her bed. Nothing in this room had been touched. There were no scent patterns to find or clues to decipher, and it was relieving in a way, because there were no other smells, no fear or blood or death.

Just Julie.

I walked over to the bookcase where a photo of us was displayed prominently. It was my high school graduation, and her dark hair was flying in the wind as I struggled to hold onto my burnt-orange graduation cap, her arm draped over my shoulder. We were both laughing, my mom snapping the candid picture that was just slightly unfocused. On another shelf was a picture of Julie and my mom at my parents' wedding—another candid—my mom in her fluffy wedding gown as the pair of them giggled at something like they had a secret.

These—and any others in the house—were the only pictures left of my parents, of me, left in the world. Sniffing, I went to Julie's closet and snagged the biggest bag I could find. A gray weekender fell off the shelf along with a couple of hat boxes, but I didn't care.

"What are you doing?" Bastian asked, having followed me at some point. His voice was kind in a way that hurt.

I refused to answer him. Instead, I shoved the picture frame in the bag. Crouching, I yanked a photo album off the shelf, flipped through it briefly, and shoved it into the bag. I found three other albums, pilfering those, too, before moving to a jewelry box on her vanity table.

Julie had plenty of expensive jewelry, rubies and sapphires and diamonds glittered from the mouth of the box, but I wasn't looking for any of that. What I was on the hunt for was a cheap opal ring that couldn't have cost more than fifty bucks. It was a giant thing, spanning from the base of her finger to her first knuckle, and I'd always admired it.

She told me once when she was gone from this world, that ring would be mine.

I dug through pricey pieces before finding it at the bottom of a tangle of pearls. Unearthing the piece, I felt a sense of home in that one little bit of cheap jewelry. A sense of happiness that I didn't have before. Slipping the ring on my finger, I breathed a sigh of relief.

"All the money just sitting in that box and you pick out the cheapest piece of jewelry? You are an odd one, Sloane." Bastian's words caught me off guard, pulling my gaze to him.

He stood with his shoulder perched on the doorframe, his arms crossed. He was studying me like he was going to be tested on what he found, his gaze roving over the room, over me, over the ring on my middle finger. Julie had always worn it on her left hand, but since I was left-handed, it went on my right.

"That other stuff isn't mine. I mean, neither are the pictures, but there is no one left to care if I take them. That ring, though, was promised to me. It seems greedy to take the other stuff."

"Like I said, you are an odd one. You could pawn that jewelry and have a tidy nest egg, but to you, that's stealing. I kind of like that about you—that you'd take the sentimental things, even though you have nothing else in the world. I was wrong about you."

Was I supposed to say thank you? I settled on shrugging and staring at my feet.

A startled yell came from downstairs, sending a thrill of unease through me.

And then the pungent scent of smoke filled my nostrils before all the windows in the room blew in.

18

Smoke filled the bedroom, flames blanketing the curtains and quickly reaching for the ceiling. But that wasn't exactly why I couldn't breathe at present. No, I couldn't breathe because a mountain of a man was currently trying to shield me from no-longer-flying glass, even though I would heal a hell of a lot faster than he would.

"Get off me," I croaked, resisting the urge to shove him off. *Idiot.* I thought it, but didn't say it, trying to conserve the little oxygen in the room. The absolute last thing I needed was me getting all vampy. It was bad enough I could smell the siren call of his blood over the acrid smoke.

Bastian moved off my back, snagging me by the back of my suit and hauling me up. He tucked me under one of his huge arms, moving me bodily as he searched for the exit. His grip was ironclad as he hauled me out of the room—well, until I yanked myself out of his hands.

"I can walk," I growled, landing on my own two feet. "Find the others. Get out of here."

Bastian shouted a protest, coughing from the smoke, but I was too busy heading back into the inferno that used to be Julie's bedroom. I couldn't leave the pictures behind. With a single-minded mission—that I knew was foolhardy but could not stop—I snagged the bag full of pictures. Fire danced close to the duffle, the flames spreading fast. I snatched the handle before spinning back to the hallway.

The scent of the flames, their heat brought back a niggle of a memory, the thought as ephemeral as the smoke dancing in the air. It was there and gone before I could grab it. Growling at myself I pressed on, trying not to breathe the acrid fumes.

Bastian was halfway down the stairs before he seemed to realize he could go no farther, the downstairs a raging inferno of odd-colored flames. They weren't orange or yellow or any other color I would have thought a flame would be. I'd never seen a green flame before, and despite the fact that it was immeasurably pretty, I knew that magical flames or not, I'd still be a crispy critter if we didn't get the fuck out of here pronto.

I swallowed hard, trying not to think of the team members we left on this floor, while sending a prayer up to any deity that would hear me that they managed to get out intact.

Bastian's own power rose on the air, orange flames coating his fingers as he seemed to press on the magical fire with his ability. Not that it did a whole hell of a lot of good. His magic seemed to make the fire grow instead of diminish, the flames growing hotter second by second.

"There's not enough water in the air to douse the flames, and my magic can't mingle with whatever this is. We need to find another way out." Bastian choked out.

And then it was me hauling him up and away from the flames, guiding him to another room that seemed less smokey. We'd have to jump from a window. If we could even get to one.

There was no doubt in my mind that this was an attack.

Oh, what gave it away, Sloane? Was it all the windows blowing in at once or the magical Molotov cocktail?

I rolled my eyes at myself, praying I remembered the layout of this house correctly. Julie's storage room had a false wall. I'd found it once and got stuck in the attic when I was seven. The attic had a line of transom windows that might have been missed in the blast. They weren't the biggest of windows, but I knew Bastian and I together were strong enough to rip the wall apart if need be.

We just needed a break from the flames.

The storage room was filled with smoke, the wall hidden behind the clutter of a well lived-in house. A sewing table with half a quilt abandoned on its top, crafting supplies, stacks of books and journals and all the things I wished I could go through, but couldn't save. The false wall hissed as I pressed on it, the cool brick a welcome sign in the blisteringly hot room.

"Help me," I ordered, and the pair of us shoved the wall to the side, revealing a wooden staircase. I grabbed Bastian's hand, yanking him behind me before I froze, realizing I'd set the bag down when I shoved the wall aside and almost went back for it. Bastian's hand tightened, stopping me.

"I got it," he yelled over the roar of the flames, holding up the leather bag like he was a harried husband at a crowded mall.

Yes, I was totally going to risk my life—and already had once—to keep those memories. Call me crazy if you want to, but it was the last vestige of my old life and I was keeping it.

Bastian overtook me on the stairs, hauling me behind him as he headed for refuge from the flames. The transom windows were larger than I'd expected, the unbroken glass big enough to fit our bodies through.

If we could reach them.

The attic space was outfitted like a safe room, full of comfy furniture, and a small kitchenette set up like one day the zombies would storm Tennessee and we'd need to hide out to avoid the horde.

"Come on, I'll help you up." He handed me the duffle.

I scoffed. "Yeah, and how will you get up there?" I pointed to the eleven-foot-high transom, the skinny window offering a teensy ledge that no one without a preternaturally skilled body could ever hope to climb.

"Don't argue, and just for once, try to listen to me. I can get out, but not if you're still in this mess. So, for fuck's sake, just let me bloody help you up, woman."

How was I supposed to argue with that?

"Fine," I grumbled. "But if you don't make it out, I will have Simon contact your ghost just so I can kick your ass. You got me?"

"Yes, yes." Bastian bent down, cradling his hands so I could use them as a step. "You'll be terribly heartbroken if I perish."

I looped an arm through the duffle handle, swinging it behind me and completely ignored Bastian's makeshift step. I took three steps back and ran straight at the wall, using my momentum to help me scale the brick. Reaching the window was the easy part, hauling myself up after unlatching it? Not so much. After shimmying my ass into position, I realized that I had the harder job.

I managed to squeeze through the window, spotting Thomas and Axel on the side lawn.

"Here," I called down to Thomas. "Catch." I shoved the duffle through the window, and it landed with a soft thump in his waiting arms.

"Now you, kid," he whisper-yelled, trying to avoid waking the neighbors before we could get the hell out of there.

I shook my head, signaling for them to wait and ducked back into the attic. "Time to go. I think everyone else is out, so come the fuck on. It's going to take the both of us to break this damn brick."

Bastian rolled his eyes at me. "I'm a mage, you silly woman. I can break the wall all on my lonesome. Just—"

"Are we having a meeting?" Thomas broke in, landing almost silently on the high pitch of the roof and scaring the shit out of me. "Or can we exit the current raging inferno that is this house?"

"Sure thing, Thomas. As soon as you convince macho man here that he needs a hand up because there is no fucking way he can scale the damn wall by himself."

Thomas gave us both a stiff nod before he latched a

hand to the window ledge and ripped the whole wall away with his bare hand like he was shredding tissue paper. It took two swipes, but there was a Bastian-sized hole in the side of Julie's house.

"Now can we go?" Thomas quipped before jumping off the roof, landing neatly on the lawn with zero problems.

The last time I'd jumped from this high, my whole body had hurt for a week. It figured Thomas could pull off a superhero landing, the bastard.

"Oh, come on, Sloane," Bastian teased, emerging from the giant hole in Julie's house and looping an arm around my waist. "It's only three stories, you wimp."

With that little quip, he shoved off the side of the house, hurtling us toward the ground. But Bastian landed with way more finesse than I had ever accomplished, absorbing the impact with ease.

I ignored Bastian's dig at my totally healthy fear of jumping off a freaking building. "Emrys and Dahlia?"

Axel answered, seeming to slide out of the shadows like a ghost. "Waiting by the truck. Let's get out of here before the fire department shows up."

I would have followed, but magic was in play and this wasn't some rinky-dink little house fire.

"Are normal firemen equipped to deal with this

shit?" I gestured to the green flames that were now licking up the brand-new hole in the attic.

Bastian snorted like I said something funny. "No, but by the time they get here, Emrys and Dahlia will have completed the break?" He said it like a question to Thomas who gave him a sharp nod. "They were just waiting until you got out. Backlash is a bitch, you know."

Backlash?

"Come on, ya'll, the sirens are getting close," Axel advised, leading us around the other side of the house where Emrys and Dahlia were walking around a circle of salt.

The pair of them began chanting in Latin once we rounded the corner, the evidence of our exit all they needed to get started. I felt the faint tremor of the ground shaking underfoot as their chanting got louder, nearly drowned out by the approaching siren. Emrys' palms began to glow as she held them aloft, her magic growing as her voice got louder. When she brought her palms down, the ground pitched in earnest, nearly knocking us all off our feet. Then the flames morphed from green to orange, their heat diminishing.

"Time to go," Bastian reminded us, but I couldn't quit staring at the orange flames that were destroying my last good memories, my last safe place.

It hit me then that Julie's home was never going to be a sanctuary ever again. Never was I going to sit at her table with a glass of wine as I bitched about Mom not understanding art or Dad not wanting me to live on campus. She would never hear me complain about Mom being so adamant about not having social media or giggle with me about some boy I maybe kind of liked but was too nervous to go talk to. She wouldn't give me a hug and a cookie and tell me I was smart to dump that guy or say goodbye to a mean person I thought was a friend. She wouldn't slide art supplies to me under the table—with Mom watching like we were hilarious—when I'd overspent my supplies budget.

This house held so many memories, and they were dying one ember at a time.

Bastian snagged my hand, but I pulled it back. I backed away from him, my eyes still on the house, even as I headed for the alley. They could go if they wanted to, but I had somewhere else to be. Reluctantly, I turned from the house as I picked up speed.

There was someplace else I needed to visit.

19

The quiet of Meadows Street didn't quite have the same safety that I'd remembered as a child. I'd learned to ride my bike on this block. I'd been pulled down the street by Otis after he caught sight of a squirrel and decided dragging me bodily on the pavement was the best way to catch it. Mrs. Blumenthal fixed me up and helped me limp back to the house. She even gave me a cookie and called my mom to come get Otis because there was no way I was going to chase him down.

My father and I fixed Mr. Ahuja's fence together after that freak thunderstorm two years ago and his kids couldn't come up from Nashville to take care of it. Mr. Rosehill had the best lawn on the block, but was in a war of attrition with Mrs. Gagne over the state of her sycamore tree.

I knew every house. Every neighbor. I knew their pets' names, their kids. I'd lived here my whole life.

But the street felt colder, more somber. The holiday lights had been taken down on all the houses, even though it was the second week in January, and the lack of twinkling lights made the air bitter and the street feel darker.

Then I saw the builder sign in what used to be my front yard, the slap in the face of my memories being destroyed again almost too much to bear. The ruined house was little more than blackened toothpicks, but it still stung that even those would soon be no more. Soon, every single thing I had of my childhood would be gone, and another house would be in its place as if we were never here. As if my father never mowed that lawn. As if my mom never watered the geraniums, or I never swung from the tire in the old oak.

As if our tiny little family were gone forever with nothing to show for it but a trio of tombstones that no one would ever visit.

I twisted the ring on my middle finger, astounded it survived my jaunt through Julie's burning house. I'd never been happier to have a single bit of jewelry in my life. Hell, my ears weren't even pierced. But that one lone ring with its cheap silver band and glittering stone made me feel just a tiny bit less lost.

A teensy bit less alone—even if it was bittersweet.

The score of a single hot tear blazed down my cheek, cooling instantly in the frigid air. I wiped it away with the back of my hand, wishing I were stronger. Wishing I was able to handle all this without turning weepy. Where was the badass who killed without remorse? I'd pay to have her back.

"Now is not the time to wander off, Sloane," a familiar British voice called.

I chuckled mirthlessly. "Any idiot with a working brain cell could figure out where I'd go, Sparky."

Bastian stepped closer, but I didn't look at him. Instead, I stared at the remains of my childhood home, my body decided more tears were the course of action. Stupid tear ducts.

"Exactly. Meaning, that if someone is going around setting fire to places you're in, maybe you shouldn't be alone." His voice was pitched low like a whisper, the wind carrying it away as the heat of him seeped into my skin, even from a foot away.

"Or maybe I should be by myself. I spent a whole year with no one trying to blow me up. One excursion with you lot and it's Molotov central." I tipped my chin back to give him a sideways glance. "You get burned?"

Bastian shook his head. "I'm mostly fireproof. Smoke inhalation, though, will get you every time."

Shifting my gaze back to the burned house, I let myself say goodbye to it. My parents weren't here—I wasn't here. The memories that I had were mine and no one could steal them. Even if so many were clouded in the truths they withheld, my life—our lives—had been wonderful. They gave me every single bit of normalcy and happiness, packing in all the years I had them.

"What if the person who burned Julie's house down did it to us, too? To hide evidence, or to kill us, or..." I shrugged. For what purpose, though? That was what was driving me crazy. *Why?*

Why burn our house down? Why kill us? What were they after? And why was Julie targeted? It was connected, I just couldn't figure out how.

"It's crossed my mind. What was in that house they didn't want us to find?"

I nodded, shivering as the cold began seeping into my bones. Bastian threw an arm over my shoulders, sharing his warmth.

I swallowed hard, gearing up for a hard question. "Do you think they would be ashamed of me? For killing like I do? For..." *The souls I've stolen?* "The things I've done?"

Bastian's arm tightened, pulling me around and to

him as he gave me an honest-to-god hug. I hadn't had one of those in a long time. As tall as he was, my head fit just under his chin, and took the likely rare opportunity to rest my cheek on his chest and absorb the warmth he was offering. I was under no illusion that we were friends—or that he even liked me for that matter—but the touch was welcome as was the comfort.

"I think," he began, but paused as he rested his cheek on top of my head, "that if they knew how many lives you've saved, how many bad people you've taken off the streets, they would be proud. You are not greedy or malicious, Sloane. And that's something—with power like ours—that has to be taught. You had a discipline of right and wrong drilled into you from your first breath. There is no way they could ever be ashamed of you. Ever."

Jesus, who the fuck was cutting onions out here?

I sniffed, tears falling down my face in earnest now. "A simple 'no' would have sufficed. You didn't have to get all mushy on me," I muttered, disgruntled that my tears refused to stay in my eyes were they damn well belonged. "You wouldn't lie about that, would you? About my parents, I mean?"

Bastian gently hooked a finger under my chin, pulling it around so I would look him in the eyes. His were a blazing green threaded through with swirls of glowing gold. "No. I would not." He shook his head slowly, never breaking our locked gaze. "Not about that. Not ever. Do you understand me?"

"Not really," I blurted honestly, and a grin broke out on his face in answer. "But don't worry. There's lots of things I don't understand."

He started chuckling in earnest, the laugh still on his lips as he dropped them to mine. For some reason I wasn't prepared for him to kiss me, the shock of his affection freezing me to the spot. This kiss felt so different from our earlier one. Less frenzied, less angry. It wasn't about feeding or the blood or the thoughts I gleaned from him.

He kissed me because he wanted to. Because he needed to. I felt as much from his touch, the truth in it washing over me as his breath mingled with mine. His giant hands cupped my face, cradling it like it was a precious treasure and then I unfroze, the softness of that touch thawing me into action.

Somehow, I found my hands covering his wrists, the strength and power in them surrounding me with a safety I hadn't felt since I woke up on the dirt a year ago. And despite my misgivings, despite Simon's warnings, despite all the bullshit I spewed to Axel about not going there, I parted my lips and let him in.

Heat enveloped my whole body, a flash fire of want

slamming into me as his tongue slid against mine. This wasn't tainted like I'd worried his earlier kisses were— this was a need, pure and simple. Bastian walked me backward until I was pushed against the rough bark of a tree, likely Mrs. Gagne's sycamore. I reveled in the pressure, the weight of his body pressing against mine as our tongues dueled for dominance. His hand fisted in my short hair, and he pulled my mouth from his as he veered south, his lips landing on the tender skin of the underside of my jaw. I shuddered as that flash fire turned into an inferno of need, his answering growl sending me into a tailspin.

Then I was up, my back still pressed against the tree, but now my legs somehow found themselves around his waist, his lips never leaving my skin as he nibbled and kissed and wound me up until I was clawing at him like a woman starved.

I could feel my fangs lengthen, the hunger rising along with my desire, but I didn't want to bite him. I wanted to feel him this way, not the secrets hidden in his blood. I wanted this mindless base need, wanted to taste his lust on the air as his scent filled my nose, wanted all of it enveloping me in all that was Bastian because it felt so much better than anything else I'd experienced ever.

A faint buzzing sound came from his pocket, but the

pair of us ignored it, his lips finding mine once again as his evident arousal pressed against my center. I couldn't help it, I moaned into his mouth. His answering groan radiated through me, the vibration waking up every millimeter of my skin, every bit of me.

The buzzing came again, and then I heard Harper's voice over comms—the first of the night.

"What did I say about that shit?" Harper growled, the tinny sound coming from Bastian's earpiece. "And answer your fucking phone, dumbass, before I figure out how to make the damn thing electrocute you."

"Anyone ever tell you that you were the mother of all cock blocks, Harper?" I asked, out of breath and pouting as Bastian let me slide down his front until I was back on two feet.

"Yeah, well, it's a specialty of mine," she sounded off in my ear, the bitter note in her tone making me feel like an asshole.

"Where have you been? You went dark for so long, you missed the attack, subsequent fire, and our daring escape. What happened?" Bastian asked, his smooth voice unhindered like mine was.

"I just got comms up after the whole compound went dark. Even the backups went offline. And something weird happened. Are you—is Simon with you?"

I moved to step away, but Bastian's arm banded

around my back, and I was once again plastered to his front. He flashed me a blindingly white smile, knowing I was a put-out disgruntled mess and not giving that first fuck. It was a blissful sort of smile that did weird things to my middle. Weird things I was not at all prepared to feel.

"Right now, no." Bastian squeezed me, his smile growing wider.

"Did he go on the mission with you?"

Bastian sighed. "You know better than that. Why are you asking?"

Harper groaned, her voice wary for maybe the first time since I'd met her, a tone I figured she didn't use all too often. "Because I can't find him. One second everything was fine, and then the house went dark and I felt this blip of emotion that… I can't find him, Bastian, and I don't know what to do."

Bastian's smile froze. Hell, his whole body froze. Then he was moving double-time, my hand in his as he dragged me behind him, heading back the way we'd come.

"Don't move, Harper," he growled, his voice like sandpaper. "I'm coming."

20

Bastian's grip was ironclad as he practically ran to the SUV, dragging me behind him. The vehicle was parked around the corner with the whole gang inside, half of them appearing to be sleeping. Bastian pounded on the glass, startling Axel who was snoozing at the wheel.

"You got Harper on comms?" he asked once Axel rolled down the window, panic radiating from his entire body.

Axel shook his head, and Emrys leaned forward to get a better view of us, her odd reddish eyes casting an eerie glow.

"What's wrong?" A flash of concern appeared on her face before it was walled behind the calm façade she usually had in place, but her eyes gave away her emotions just like mine did.

Bastian practically vibrated, he was so wound up. "Harper said comms went offline after a power outage at the house. Full black out, battery and auxiliary power wiped out. She felt a blip of emotion before it was gone, and now she can't find Simon. Power is back online, but..."

Thomas rolled down his window. "Get in the truck, you idiots." He fished an earpiece out of a pocket and stuck it in his ear. "Harper? Can you locate him with his phone or the GPS in his car?"

Harper's scathing voice came over comms as Bastian and I climbed into the back of the SUV. "I would if they weren't right fucking here just like *he's* supposed to be. Don't you think I thought of that? Would I worry every single member of the team unnecessarily, dipshit?"

"Harper?" Emrys cooed, her voice in stereo in the car and on comms. "Take a breath for me. If you can't find him by conventional means, then Dahlia or I will locate him. You are doing all the right things, sweetheart."

The thought of Emrys calming Harper down reminded me of my own mother, the way she would cheer me on when we went on our family hikes, the way she would push me. I liked that Harper had that even if I didn't.

We settled in our seats, and all the while Bastian hadn't let go of my hand. I squeezed his fingers so he knew I was there for him. Simon was Bastian's weak spot, and I wasn't going to let him worry alone. He gave me a quick squeeze back, but didn't look at me, his eyes forward as Axel navigated the sleepy streets.

Harper's exhale breezed through my ear.

"Good girl," Emrys murmured. "Now, lock yourself in your room. We're coming to you. Have you seen Booth?"

"No," Harper answered, "But I didn't look for him. He's supposed to be healing up, right? I figured he'd still be passed out after Axel's drug cocktail of painkillers."

Axel snorted, the SUV accelerating through the dark night, the speed limit a mere suggestion to be ignored. "I gave that boy enough to put down an elephant after Thomas got done beating on him. If he isn't howling for more drugs, he should be dead to the world. Don't you worry none about Booth."

Harper exhaled again, relief in that little puff of air, but I was confused. Why would Thomas beat on Booth? Was it because of me? Because he'd bitten me? Was that what Axel had meant?

"Okay," she whispered. "I'll sit tight. I won't worry about what I can't change. I'll wait for you guys to get here." She said it like she was telling herself rather than reassuring us.

"Good work, Short Stack," Axel crooned through the earpiece. "We'll be there in two shakes of a lamb's tail. Don't you worry about a thing."

Axel flicked the earpiece out of his ear, tightened his grip on the wheel, and pressed the gas to the floor—or at least that's what it seemed like after I was shoved back in my seat from the force. I wasn't the only one who knew something was really wrong, but no one was saying it. So I kept my mouth shut and hoped Simon was going to be okay.

We screamed down the manicured driveway and screeched to a stop in the garage—barely missing a very sleek street bike with an armored guard on the gas tank. We piled out, Axel and Thomas making silent hand gestures at each other before peeling off.

Bastian hadn't said a word in the minutes since we'd explained the problem, and the longer we went on without word from Simon, the more rigid his back got. His neck muscles were so tight, if he tried to move his head, he'd break his whole fucking spine.

Emrys put a hand on Bastian's elbow, stopping him. "Bastian, I want you to go find Clem, make sure she has something to do before she goes bananas. Have her make his favorite or something." He peeled off, likely grateful for something to do. "Sloane, I want you to stay with Dahlia while I collect what I need and get Harper. Do not leave her side, you got me?"

It felt like she was asking me to guard Dahlia for some reason, and I was more than happy to have a job to do. I felt useless, my knowledge of the house limited, meaning I couldn't help Axel and Thomas with the perimeter check. I couldn't do magic, so I was not needed there. After the fire, I really needed something to do that I was good at, and bodyguard was as good a thing as any. I really wished I could see Simon's room, but that wasn't what she'd asked, so I didn't suggest it.

"Yes, ma'am," I answered, and she was gone, moving so fast I almost lost track of her. Emrys wasn't as fast as Thomas, but she could *move*.

I turned to Dahlia. For the mission, she'd had her braids gathered in a loose bun at the nape of her neck, but she was setting them free. She cracked her neck, her entire body restless as the tension and silence grew.

"You okay?" I asked stupidly. It was obvious she wasn't fine, but I needed to get her talking. She hadn't said a word since before the fire, and I was worried she might be going into shock. Or maybe that was her "mission mode."

Dahlia looked at me, really looked at me for maybe the first time since we got to Aunt Julie's house. Her eyes were wild, fear dancing in them as she seemed to be struggling to keep it all in. "Simon isn't supposed to leave the property—not after he made Clem. If he left— if he..." She shook her head, her teeth pressing into her bottom lip. "There would be no reason we couldn't find him unless someone took him."

"Made Clem? Is that against the rules or something?"

Dahlia nodded. "He was supposed to kill her. Necromancy—well, all death magic—is highly regulated. Reanimating a body, filling it with a spirit? He popped up on a radar he should have avoided. Emrys used all her pull to keep him out of trouble, but he was put on house arrest."

I shook my head. "By who?"

"The ABI. It was all Emrys could do to keep him out of their clutches. Simon wouldn't just leave. He only has a month left on his sentence."

I only very recently discovered there was such a thing as the Arcane Bureau of Investigation, and their scope was still unclear to me. "How long has he been stuck here?"

"Ten years. Simon has been locked down for ten years and he only has a month left. Or *had*." Dahlia began pacing, her long braids swishing against her back as she pivoted. "If it's something stupid and he's not here, I'm going to freaking kill him."

Dahlia was still pacing when Emrys and Harper returned, both of their arms loaded down with spell ingredients. Dahlia hefted a vase off the round entryway table, and Emrys shook out a dark purple cloth that had golden moon designs printed on the fabric. Harper set pillar candles in exact intervals and handed Dahlia a metal bowl and a map.

Emrys turned to me. "Do me a favor, will you? Look over Simon's room. Sniff around, look for clues."

I had a feeling she was either giving me something to do or wanted me gone. But I wasn't going to argue with her—especially since that was all I'd wanted to do since I stepped foot in the house.

Taking the stairs two at a time, I reached Simon's room in a flash. I didn't know much about Simon other than he was Bastian's brother. Well, that and he was apparently a death mage with a skeleton cat and a penchant for pissing off the ABI. Simon's room wasn't much different from the last time I'd been in there. A battered couch in front of an unmade bed, gaming controllers strewn about. Books littered tabletops and nightstands and parts of the floor, some open, some in haphazard stacks that could topple at any moment. The dark curtains were drawn, and a lamp sat lit on an end table with its shade slightly off-kilter. A giant TV was mounted against the wall, a slight film of dust over the dark screen.

On the high-pile rug in front of the TV was a spirit board, but not the cardboard and plastic kid's game one would pick up at a big box store. No, this was a solid-wood affair with hand-carved letters and runes etched around the edges, along with a pair of skulls. The planchet appeared to be made of an iridescent shell of some kind, with a glittering glass viewer. Next to it was a pad and a pen half-covered with a dirty shirt.

But it was the scent that permeated the room that really caught my attention. Beneath the scent of dirty laundry and a stale pizza that had probably been shoved under his bed and forgotten, was the faint traces of the people who had been in this room. Bastian was a mainstay, his masculine flavor all over a battered reading chair. Dahlia, too, she had a favorite side of the couch and her floral bouquet infused that space.

It wasn't those scents on top of Simon's that concerned me.

It was Booth's.

It was fresh, barely an hour old, but it was still here. And that's when a few things became frighteningly clear. Even with Axel in Julie's house, I barely smelled him, but Booth's signature was everywhere. On her couch, on the air, still clinging to everything. If there had been anyone else in that house, I would have known, as much as they touched, as much damage as they caused, there would have been some trace left behind.

But there wasn't. I only smelled Booth and Julie.

A hot pit of dread opened wide in my belly. I couldn't say why I strode forward to look at the pad of paper. Couldn't say why I peeled the T-shirt back to see the message I knew was written on it.

Beware of Booth. Tell Sloane I love her.

My hand shook as I reached for the pad, a sheen of tears in my eyes blurring the page.

Aunt Julie.

He'd contacted Julie and she'd told him to be careful.

Booth's scent was the only one in Julie's house besides hers.

Beware of Booth.

21

Hot tears fell down my cheeks as I nearly crushed the paper in my hand.

Beware of Booth.

My lips trembling, I backed slowly away from the board.

Did he kill Julie? Did he kill her and then come here and look at me like he'd done nothing wrong, like *I* was the wolf in *his* midst. Did he bite into me knowing he'd tasted her flesh, knowing he'd killed the very last bit of my family?

But Booth had been a wolf when we'd trained. Not a cat.

I vaguely remembered Dahlia's instruction on shifters—that they could turn into any animal—but I couldn't remember if Booth was a shifter or a were.

I had to tell the others. Even if I was wrong—not that I thought I was—Booth had to be located. As far as I knew no one had checked on him, assuming he was still laid up from Thomas' *instruction*. Whatever that meant.

"What's in your hand?" Bastian asked, and I whirled, my whole body trembling in fear, and knowledge. "What's wrong?"

Slowly, I held my hand out to him, showing him the message Simon had jotted down from the spirit board, unable to tell him all the thoughts swirling in my head.

"It was next to a spirit board. And this whole room smells like Booth. Just like Julie's house. There wasn't another shifter there. I only smelled Booth." I'd thought when I found the person responsible for taking Julie from me, I'd be cold, methodical. I thought it wouldn't burn every single bit of me like I was dying, the loss of her hitting me in new ways. But I wasn't calm, I wasn't collected.

I was a mass of fury and rage and fear and grief. I was barely holding myself together.

"He isn't here, is he? Tell me someone checked on him. Tell me he's here and this is just one big mistake," I challenged him, waiting for him to meet my gaze, waiting for him to tell me I was wrong.

Bastian swallowed, his hazel eyes finally meeting

mine. I saw the truth in them, the widened gaze that held the signature of fear.

"Come on. We'll find them. It has to be a misunderstanding. It has to be," he offered, reaching for my hand, but I backed away.

"He killed her. He killed my only family," I whispered. "He took your brother. Why? Why did he do this to us? What did we ever do to him?"

Bastian stepped into my space, his hands cradling my face as he stared in my eyes. "We don't know that, Sloane. Let's tell the others what you've found. Maybe we're wrong."

Maybe we're wrong.

He believed me and didn't want to. I knew why, too. Bastian wanted to believe there was hope for Simon, hope that he would be alive and whole, and unharmed. That this was one big mistake, and we weren't delaying all the grief that was threatening to crash over our heads.

Because if Booth killed Julie, what was stopping him from killing Simon? If he was a monster, was there a rhyme or reason to his murders, or did he kill indiscriminately?

Hesitantly, I gave him a trembling nod and let him guide me out of the room. My fear for Simon ramped up when I heard Dahlia's frustrated groan. Over the banister, I spied the whole gang grouped around the table, the candles alight and casting an odd glow on them all.

"Why can't I find him?" she growled, and the fear that was threatening to crash into me began to crest. The candles that dotted the edge of the table winked out, their flames dying with the end of her spell.

"I think we've got something," Bastian called, pulling me behind him down the stairs. He thrust the pad into Emrys' hands, his rage crinkling the paper. "This was by his spirit board."

Beware of Booth. Tell Sloane I love her.

That message would be burned into my brain until the end of time.

It took Emrys less than a second to read the paper, her trembling hand giving it away, but she didn't raise her head. "Thomas? Check that Booth is where you left him, will you?"

Thomas' eyes widened, his sclera reddening almost instantly. He gave her a swift nod that I doubted she saw before he was gone. His rage-filled scream not a moment later was answer enough. Booth wasn't here.

That didn't explain why Dahlia couldn't find Simon, though. Unless he was...

"What's going on?" Dahlia asked, and Emrys showed her the paper. The message was powerful enough that speaking it aloud would brand us all.

Dahlia pressed a hand to her chest like she was holding in her heart. Like if she moved wrong, if she took her hand away, her heart would shatter into a million pieces. She stood like that for one long moment before she took a shuddering breath. A single tear fell down her face, and then her expression turned to stone, her jaw visibly clenching.

"None of this explains why I can't find him. Dead or alive, in the next room or in Timbuktu, I should be able to find his skinny ass no matter where it is. Where the fuck is he?"

Emrys offered a comforting squeeze to Dahlia's shoulder, but the witch shrugged it off. I understood not wanting comfort in a time like this. "Maybe he's being cloaked?"

"By Booth?" Bastian scoffed. "Not likely. This is bigger than Booth, I can feel it."

"What about Clem?" I asked, falling onto a nearby chair situated next to a bookcase. "You said he made her, right? Wouldn't the magic in her body be like a link to him or something?"

I knew little about spells or magical items—even less about death magic—but I knew enough about magical bonds to fill a whole library. Every arcaner had a blood tie to their maker or parent. Lycanthropes had one to the arcaner who'd bitten them. Ghouls had one to the death mage who raised them. Vampires to their sire.

If Clem was a spirit inhabiting a reanimated body, she was essentially created by Simon, and should have a link to him in her blood. If she even had blood in her veins. That was definitely suspect, but it was all I had.

Emrys turned to Axel, her hand on his arm. "Ask her if she's willing. Convince her if need be."

I doubted Clem would need convincing, but I didn't say anything.

A quiet meow had me staring at the floor, Isis sat at my feet, and I picked her up, setting the bone kitty on my lap. She rested her head on my chest, fully leaning into me like she needed me to support her this time instead of the other way around.

"I can't purr at you," I told her. "But I can give scratches. We'll find him, sweet girl."

The swish of the kitchen door sounded before Clem appeared in the dining room doorway. Flour covered one deathly pale cheek as well as her black apron which spelled out "Drop Dead Gorgeous" in a glittery purple curlicue font. She marched her way over like a woman on a mission, her odd, icy-blue eyes sharp as a razor as she stomped right up to Bastian.

She seemed like she wanted to slap the shit out of him but managed to hold herself back by the skin of her teeth. "You knew he was gone, and you had me making him apple dumplings instead of helping, you dumb fuck? I ought to kick your simple mage ass up and down this house. I am not some fragile little flower, you macho moron, and you'd better get that into your thick skull before I beat it into you."

Clem then swiftly turned on her heel and marched right to Dahlia on her sky-high heels, dismissing Bastian with a swish of her emerald skirt.

I wanted to hold in my snicker, but with all the stress, with all that had happened in the last two days, I just couldn't. I cuddled Isis closer and busted up laughing, tears trickling out of my eyes as I replayed Clem's words in my head, the tirade getting funnier each time I thought about it.

"Dear sweet lord in heaven, did ya'll break her or something?" Clem asked once my giggles turned into an odd snorting guffaw.

"Or something," Bastian supplied, kneeling at my feet. He warily eyed my arms around the bone kitty, and I nearly busted out in a fit of giggles again once I remembered that Bastian was not a fan of Simon's cat.

I pressed my lips together, holding in my obviously ill-timed mirth. I mouthed a "sorry" to Bastian. Even though he had a faint smile on his lips, I still felt like an asshole. Here I was laughing like a loon while his brother was in a murderer's clutches. I needed a padded cell and an empathy chip installed.

Quickly, I sobered, my mirth dying a swift death. I released one hand free from Isis and reached for his fingers. My family was dead, but he still had Simon, and we'd need to bring him back just so Bastian wouldn't have to feel like I had every day of this past year.

So he didn't go cold like I did.

Outside of our little bubble, Dahlia and Clem were working together to find Simon, but here in this silent little space, Bastian and I held each other's hands and tried not to break down. I wanted to be wrong about Booth. I wanted Simon to be okay and this whole thing to be a misunderstanding. I wanted Bastian's worry to be for nothing.

But I knew I was simply trying to fool myself, so I held his hand and tried to think happy thoughts as I watched Dahlia work.

Dahlia lanced Clem's finger with a slim knife, collecting the slow, black blood in a small metal bowl. Clem's blood smelled of death and magic and... an earthiness I couldn't place until I remembered the day I woke up in a cemetery.

Clementine carried the scent of the grave.

Dahlia snapped her fingers and the candles all lit at once, their flames dancing high for a moment before shrinking to normal size. She dropped some herbs from a vial into the bowl with Clem's blood in it, twisting her hand as she did so. The bowl rose in the air and began spinning on its own as Dahlia dropped more and more ingredients into it—a little salt, some chalk, a drop of her own blood. She snapped her fingers again, the contents igniting in a ball of purple flames.

Clem staggered, nearly falling off her spike heels before Thomas caught her, his reemergence from his search for Booth going unnoticed in the height of the spell. But no one was looking at Thomas at all.

We were all staring at Clem.

Clem's ghostly pale face turned a shade of gray I'd only glimpsed in the long dead. Her icy eyes rolled back in her head, leaving only a white sclera as the orbs began to glow. She started convulsing in Thomas' arms, a thin ribbon of black blood dripping from her nose.

And then she began to speak, the words flowing together in a language I didn't know but sounded familiar. It wasn't Latin, but it was close.

"Blood and death call to you," Bastian translated. "Blood and death call to us all. A master of death awaits you. He awaits you in the hiding place of the soul stealer. He waits for you to bring him home."

Soul stealer? Did she just blurt out my secret all over the fucking table?

Why, yes. Yes, she did.

A flash fire of guilt and adrenaline slammed into me. I'd kind of planned on telling people that little nugget of info around about never, and Clem just spilled all the fucking tea like she was a one-woman tea-spilling machine. My heart tripped inside my chest as I tried not to flinch at Bastian's translation.

Thomas, however, could hear my heart just fine. He leaned around Clem's red victory rolls as he leveled me with a stare so sharp it was a wonder it didn't cut me in two. I cuddled Isis closer, ready and willing to use the kitty as a shield.

All the candles blew out at once, the bowl falling with a metallic clink on the table, and seven pairs of eyes followed Thomas' lead.

"Soul stealer?" Thomas prompted, his eyebrows raised as he awaited an answer.

I was so fucked.

22

In all our scant discussions of what I was, not once did Emrys mention that soul readers could also eat souls. I knew, of course, but I hadn't brought it up because I thought if they didn't know, I wasn't going to tell them. Either that, or it was too taboo a subject, and no one was going to call me out. I was sort of hoping for the second one, but I now knew it was the first.

Maybe I should have confirmed this information—at least to Emrys.

"I'm guessing that ability is not standard issue with soul readers then?" With the lack of head nods and unblinking stares, I shrunk in my seat. "Cool. Umm... Surprise?"

Harper snorted, her eyes wide. "So, you don't just read souls, you eat them?"

I winced. "Only the really bad ones?"

Bastian stood from his crouch, the height disparity not at all comforting with his stony expression. "That was why you wanted to die. Because you consumed a soul and thought what?"

"Pretty much that I was a soul-sucking monster. It was shockingly hard to take myself out, too. Jumping off buildings, getting run over by a bus, starving myself. The list goes on. The only thing I didn't try was cutting off my own head, but it's surprisingly difficult to locate a guillotine nowadays."

"And you failed to mention this at our first feeding, why again?" His lips barely moved as he spoke through a clenched jaw, bald malice and rage lighting his eyes like twin emeralds.

"Hey," I protested, shoving out of my seat, still holding the skeleton kitty. "I distinctly recall me warning that I'd kill you. But then when the feeding started, I didn't read sins in your blood. I just saw *us*. And I didn't have any desire to drain you dry, so I figured it was only really bad souls that were tasty. Still, I requested blood bags, even after both of our feedings just to be safe." I shot my gaze to Axel. "Tell him."

Axel gave me a slow nod. "She did, though she didn't say why."

"A glowing endorsement, Axel, thanks. It's not like I chose this. It's not like one day I woke up and decided, 'hey, let's devour some souls for breakfast.' I was evidently born this way." I pinched the bridge of my nose. "Look, I get that everyone has a hair up their ass about this, but we've got bigger fish to fry. Simon is gone, and if Clem is right, I know where he is. You want to try and figure out how to kill me, great. But let's do it later."

Thomas set a groggy Clem on her feet, steadying her so she didn't go down. "I've never heard of a soul reader actually consuming souls. How can this be?"

"I've heard whispers about soul readers being like you, but they seemed like fairytales," Emrys admitted. "Long ago rumblings full of nonsense meant to scare people away from interbreeding. I understand why you didn't tell us."

"Emrys—" Bastian began, but she cut him off.

"Would you tell strangers about all that Simon can do? Or about Harper? Or Clem? Would you tell them about how Axel and Thomas have been kicked out of every nest they've ever lived in? Would you feel safe enough to let them see the darkness in you? Don't lie— to me or yourself—and answer honestly. Would you?"

Bastian tilted his head back and stared at the ceiling. "No, I wouldn't. So, I should quit being a dick about it. Got it."

His admission was all well and good, but the man wouldn't look at me. I guessed I knew where we were on that front. The sting of rejection—not just from Bastian, but from everyone—washed over me, crushing me with its weight.

At least Isis still liked me.

But I couldn't rely on a cat to get me through this. I was right back to what I felt what seemed like so long ago. I shouldn't get attached to these people. I shouldn't want them to like me, shouldn't try and rely on them any more than I should the damn cat.

I stared straight ahead, no longer meeting anyone's gaze. If I did, I knew they'd see the wound they'd caused, they'd see me bleeding. How many times could my heart be broken, anyway? A handful of times? A thousand? I was once again so happy that Harper couldn't read me anymore. Happy that she couldn't feel this ache in my chest, this pit in my stomach.

Soon enough, I'd be able to turn all of it off. I'd save myself the trouble of wanting things. I'd go back to being on my own, back to the streets where at least I wasn't a burden to anyone else.

"Simon is in an old warehouse close to downtown

Ascension." I tried to get them back on task. "I can show you the place myself if you want. If not, I can draw you a map, but I'd feel better if I went along. I know the building and where all the vulnerabilities are."

I walked over to Dahlia and took the whip hilt out of my holster. "You can have this back. I know you made it for a different girl."

But Dahlia refused to take the weapon from me, pushing my hand away. "I made it for you. I don't take back gifts after they're given."

That wasn't exactly acceptance, but it didn't matter. Giving her a sharp nod, I put the hilt back in the holster. I'd leave it in the truck for her when I left.

She'd want it back eventually.

"All right then. Let's roll out in five," Emrys called. "Gather everything you need for a fight. Harper, you're staying here. Clem is given free rein to protect you, so don't sass her when she's back to rights. Engage the Ivory Tower protocol once we leave."

I had everything I technically owned on me—aside from a duffle full of pictures—so I stayed put, but Thomas, Bastian, and Axel peeled off to gather more weapons. Clem shook herself and told us she was headed to the armory. Dahlia left to grab more potion bottles, and Harper trudged upstairs grumbling about a stupid Ivory Tower protocol.

That left me and Emrys still standing at the table. For the longest moment, neither of us spoke, but she broke the tense silence with a whispered apology. "I'm sorry, Sloane. I thought… I don't know what I thought."

My smile was bitter, but I didn't meet her gaze, even though I knew she wanted me to. "I knew this place was too good for the likes of me."

"Oh, no, Sloane. We're really not. All of us have secrets like yours. All of us. Even me."

I met her eyes, tears swimming in mine. "I don't belong here, and you can say I do, but I don't. You should know—just in case I don't get to tell you—Julie saw people attacking the house before she died. They were coming to kill everyone here. At the time, I didn't know what it meant, but I think I do now. If I stay here and someone finds out what I can do, they'll come. They'll come and kill everyone because of me. Like my parents. Like Julie." I swallowed, the pain clogging my throat. "So, after we get Simon back, I'm leaving."

"No, Sloane. You don't have to do that. We'll figure something out."

I shook my head, tears falling down my face faster than I could wipe them away. "I do. You don't need me here mucking things up, and that's the end of it." I swallowed again, trying to stop crying. "I'll meet ya'll in the truck."

And then I left, following my scant memory of how to get to the garage. The SUV sat cold, and I was lucky the thing was still unlocked. I climbed in, sitting all the way in the back like I had before.

Before when Bastian had hold of my fingers.

When he gave a shit.

When I had friends.

Funny how much could change in an hour.

I'd get Simon back. I'd help. And then I'd leave with the knowledge that it would always be better if I stayed on my own. For however long it took to die.

It didn't take too long before people were piling into the SUV, the silence thick as molasses. I put my earpiece back in and looked out the window, reciting the address I knew by heart. I stared out the window and watched the world skate by as we flew down the driveway and onto the highway.

Night still held strong, as it would in this part of winter, and I relished the cold pane of glass against my forehead and the warmth of the interior of the vehicle. I tried to hold onto small comforts, tried to feel things to be thankful for. I'd learned a hard lesson. I'd had a tiny bit of happiness. I'd had a small dose of affection. I'd just have to make those moments stretch and last for however long.

When we entered the city, I began detailing the

building. The several entrances and exits, the levels. The pitfalls and booby traps. But my descriptions must not have done the building justice because both Thomas and Axel cussed a blue streak when we rolled passed.

"Are you fucking kidding me, Sloane?" Thomas railed, twisting in his seat to look at me fully. "You spent a year holed up in that dump, and you want to leave us for that? What? Is the mansion not good enough for you?"

I stared straight ahead, the knife in my heart twisting. "You know that's not why, Thomas. You said it yourself. I'm an albatross. I'm the reason you'll all get killed. You're safer without me there. Simon was safer without me there." Finally, I let my gaze meet his. "You said you owed me? Well, you can start by not making me feel like shit because you and I both know that no one wants me in your home. You didn't want me there two days ago, and you don't want me now. So let me go."

I said the words to Thomas, but they were for everyone. They were for Bastian and Dahlia and Axel who looked at me like I was a monster. They were for Harper and Emrys and Simon, too. I wasn't welcome and never would be. They'd finally learned what I'd figured out the first day into this new life. That it would have been better if I'd have just stayed dead.

In a flash, a blur of white bones jumped from the

cargo area and onto my lap. Isis curled in on herself, her odd kitty face peering at me with her glowing green eyes.

"What the hell are you doing here?" I asked, secretly relieved to have a friendly face.

Isis meowed in my face, her eyes glowing like twin moons. She reached up on her hind legs and perched her forelegs on my shoulders. Her gaze grew brighter, the green so brilliant I almost couldn't look at it. She meowed in my face again, long and low before a green mist wafted out of her mouth like curling fingers of smoke.

The smoke flowed into my nose and mouth, filling my head with images of the warehouse. She showed me where there were men guarding the entrances, where Simon was, and the biggest problem of them all.

"Booth has Simon," I breathed, my vision still in the warehouse and not in the SUV with the team. "He has him on the third floor in some kind of contraption that will shove him over the edge of the catwalk if Simon moves wrong. But that's not the bad part."

The apparition burned away until the cab came back into focus. I stared at Isis, marveling at what she'd shown me—even if it was pretty much all bad news.

"Not the bad part?" Bastian groused. "What could possibly be worse than someone we trusted holding my brother hostage? You know, other than the fact that you're getting your information from a dead feline?"

I would agree that Bastian had a point, but the bad part was way worse.

"The building is surrounded by ghouls."

Because of course it was.

23

Axel groaned before slamming the SUV to a stop and throwing it into park in an abandoned parking lot, three blocks from the building where Simon was being held. From there, he let out the mother of all growls.

"Of fucking course it is. Any other rays of sunshine you wish to bestow on me? Maybe my father has come back from the grave, or my ex-wife is finally ready to ask me for alimony. Maybe there are rabid alligators and squirrels on PCP in there, too."

As funny as Axel was in the middle of his grown-man hissy fit, I was still focused on the fact that a cat gave me a vision. "Umm... What in the actual all-encompassing fuck did I just...? Why is Isis showing me shit?"

Bastian snorted as he readjusted his weapons. "Isis is

Simon's psychopomp. A spirit guide, if you will. He must have sent her a message, and since she likes you, she gave it to you."

I ran a fingertip over her boney spine. "Aren't you a smart girl?" To the rest of them, I asked, "So this is what Simon has seen?"

Thomas turned back around, adjusting knives and weapons as well. "Simon can sense a large majority of the undead. Like most death mages, Simon knows when ghouls are near. Ghouls are the product of death mage magic, so he feels their signature. What you saw might be what he feels, or it could be a mix of what he's seen and what he senses around him."

But what Isis showed me was more than a feeling. It was as if I were flying above everyone and everything unnoticed, like I was looking through a ghost's eyes.

Simon's eyes? Was he already dead? Was this a suicide mission?

I didn't try to explain what I saw—it wasn't like we had the time—and outlined where I thought we should breach. "The third floor is where the catwalk is. If we just wanted to get Simon and get out, I'd breach on the south side where I have a pulley system integrated with the old fire escape. It's hard to get to and they might not know about the secret entry."

The building used to be an old paper factory before it

shut down about fifty years ago. The city had been trying to have it torn down for ages, but couldn't get the votes since it was still structurally sound. This wasn't where I had stayed every night—or day—but this was the place I'd gone to when I was scared. It was a place I'd fortified as best I could with scraps and leftover tools.

Yes, it was a shithole. A dump, as Thomas called it, but it was what I had when I had nothing.

That wasn't to say I'd be going back to it when I left them. I had a feeling that Ascension wasn't the place for me anymore.

Harper's voice rang out on comms. "Sloane is right, the third-floor entrance might offer you the best cover, but you should be careful. There are only two heat signatures in the factory, but I'm catching movement on the neighboring rooftops. No heat sig. Could be ghouls or vampires or both."

I wanted to ask how Harper could see the neighboring rooftops, but I decided that some things could just stay a mystery. Knowing Harper, she probably hacked into a defense satellite or something.

"I would advise attacking from the south and taking out any ghouls watching that side," Harper recommended.

"That's as good a place to start as any," Emrys conceded before letting out the mother of all sighs.

"Dahlia, you're with Thomas. Axel, you're with me. Bastian, you're with Sloane. Stay sharp. Watch each other's backs. Let's head out, people."

We piled out of the truck, and I led the group to the nearby building. The paper factory was surrounded by a handful of outbuildings, more than a handful of decommissioned warehouses and an old shoe factory. This part of Ascension was left to ruin, the city council always trying to get it wiped out but never managing to seal the deal. Only transients and the homeless hung around here now. But the humans stayed closer to the streets and away from the buildings, likely sensing the things that clung to the shadows, their hindbrains realizing they were prey.

I clung to the walls of an alley as I made my way toward a fire escape a few buildings away. No way did I want to be in an alley, bottle-necked by ghouls. Unlike vampires, ghouls were pack hunters, their strength coming in numbers rather than talons or fangs. Impossibly strong and difficult to kill, they appeared human enough that they could pass you on the street and no one would be the wiser.

Had their diet not consisted of little more than human flesh, they'd fit right in.

My biggest concern was the noise. Like vamps, ghoul hearing was near the top of the pack. It was possible they would hear us coming even from this far away, but we didn't have the time to waste. As silently as I could, I crept up the fire escape stairs, careful to avoid the rusted treads that I knew would either dump me on my ass or squeal like an angry pig. The last thing we needed was every arcaner within a mile radius to know we were here. Surprise was the only damn thing we had going for us.

Once we reached the top of the fire escape, I peered over the ledge of the roof. Immediately, I ducked back down, barely managing not to get spotted by the three huge ghouls patrolling the roof. Reluctantly, I glanced back at Bastian. He'd followed me up this set of stairs, and now we had to figure out a way to silently take these ghouls out. Well, I knew a way, but he wasn't going to like it.

I held up three fingers, telling him how many we had to deal with and pointed to their general position. He jerked his thumb to his chest and held up two fingers, indicating he'd take out two of them, leaving me to take out the third. I picked the closest one, and on his count of three, I launched myself over the ledge. It took three bounds before I was on the behemoth of a man and my fangs in his neck. I had other weapons at my disposal, but I was familiar with these.

All eight of my razor-sharp fangs buried themselves

into the ghoul's neck and I ripped, tearing out his throat before he could scream. Then it was just a one, two, twist and his head came off in my hands, his big body withering as it crumpled to the rooftop. It was unlikely he'd shrivel to ash, but at least he was really, really dead.

I looked up to see Bastian battling the second ghoul, the first a smoldering mess of flames on the ground. There were only two ways to kill a ghoul: beheading or fire. Beheading took the least amount of time and was a confirmed kill. Fire took too damn long, and if the ghoul put themselves out quick enough, then we were up shit creek. Groaning, I yanked the spelled whip out of the holster and muttered the incantation to activate it.

The electric-blue tendril of magic bloomed from the hilt, and I wasted no time launching it at the downed ghoul, wrapping it around its neck and yanking off the smoldering remains of his head. Dead checks were an important part of survival. The fact that ripping off someone's head was supremely fun was just a bonus.

Bastian and the last ghoul were circling each other, Bastian with a ball of electricity in his hand and the ghoul missing the lower half of his left arm. Still, the ghoul lunged—one and a half arms outstretched—his teeth bared. Bastian launched his electricity ball, hitting the thing right in the chest. The giant ghoul froze for a few seconds before it let out an unearthly growl and slowly stepped forward.

"Bastian," I whisper-hissed. "Duck." Bastian turned to me, his eyes wide, before he dove for the ground.

I launched the whip at the ghoul's throat, the blue magic wrapping around his neck, and the next instant, I yanked. The crackling whip cut through the ghoul's neck like butter, dropping him like a stone on the debris-strewn rooftop. This ghoul was older than the rest, his giant body crumbling to dust almost instantly. I shrugged. At least clean-up would be a breeze.

"Umm... Sloane?" Bastian called softly. "You know you're still holding a severed head, right?"

I stared down at my right hand, and it turned out Bastian was right. I was, in fact, holding a withering head. *Gross.* Immediately, I dropped the head like its hair was on fire, wiping my fingers on my pants. I suppressed a shudder at the utter ick factor and whispered the incantation to retract the whip before holstering it.

"This building is clear," Bastian muttered through comms. "We're on a higher floor than the surrounding buildings, so it's possible no one saw our little debacle."

"Except me," Harper said in my ear. "I know I saw it, but Sloane, did you really just rip that ghoul's head off with your bare hands?"

Wasn't that how everyone did it? It wasn't like I had a sword in my hand to ease the job along.

"Status update," Bastian barked, surreptitiously looking over the side of the ledge to see the building below. I followed suit, peeking over the crumbling brick. Even with upgraded vision, I couldn't make out much despite the full moon casting a decent light on an empty rooftop. But I knew better. It had been my experience that ghouls were masters of the shadows, able to blend in and stay hidden, unmoving for hours.

I *hated* hunting ghouls.

Harper grumbled about him spoiling her fun but gave us a quick briefing. "Emrys and Axel have cleared the rooftops on the building to the west. Dahlia and Thomas to the east. There is one more building to clear to the south, and then you have a straight shot to the factory. Since the factory ceiling is mostly glass, I doubt any ghouls are waiting up there, but I don't know about the inside. Footage is not pulling up any movement."

"Can you see Simon?" I asked. "He should be visible on the catwalk, depending on your vantage point."

"That's a negative," Harper replied. "I can't see past the full moon's reflection on the glass."

Fabulous.

"Okay, ladies and gents," Axel called over comms, "converge on the southern rooftop. I see seven ghouls and what looks like a couple of lycanthropes. Do not, I repeat, do not get bitten. I only have one anti-viral in my pack, and I'm saving it just in case Simon needs it."

I wondered if I should tell him I was immune to the lycanthrope virus. Nah, I'd wait to share that little tidbit if I got snacked on.

"Let's move, people," Emrys commanded, and we did.

Bastian rose from his crouch and walked away from the ledge. I followed suit, wondering what the hell he thought he was doing. Yes, the other rooftop was close, but not close enough to jump, and he seemed like he was getting ready to do just that.

"What are you doing?" I hissed, knowing full well what his answer was going to be.

Bastian rolled his eyes. "I'm jumping—what's it look like? You are, too, you wimp."

I shook my head. "I've already dove off one building, thank you. The healing took forever. That roof is over forty feet away. You can't make that jump. I don't care if you think you're a freaking superhero."

A ghost of a smile stretched over his lips before he latched onto my waist, securing me to his side. "Sure I can. You can, too."

Then he took off, running full tilt for the ledge like a crazy person.

24

I almost screamed but refused to give our position away. Instead, I shut my eyes tight as we sailed over the side of the building, trying desperately not to freak the fuck out. The closest I came to death in this new life was when I jumped off a building. The subsequent fear of falling—well, not to my death because if twenty stories didn't do it, nothing would— was a very real thing.

But gravity didn't work the same way as it had on that rather mournful night. The pull wasn't nearly as strong, and it wasn't a moment later that our feet landed heavily on the rooftop, our momentum leading us into a skid. When I opened my eyes, the fight was in full bloom, and I quickly realized that Axel's numbers were off. There weren't seven ghouls, there were twenty, and there were a hell of a lot more lycanthropes than a few.

A full concentric ring of half-man, half-wolf lycanthropes stood on the outskirts of the melee, their misshapen mouths snapping in anticipation. Dahlia was snapping her fingers, popping heads off like it was a piece of cake. Thomas was swiftly taking ghoul heads with a pair of broad swords that he pulled from who knew where. He sure as shit wasn't wearing them the last time I saw him. Emrys was throwing spells, her glowing hands sending shockwaves to the ghouls to knock them down as Axel took what appeared to be a spelled garrote to the ones that landed at his feet.

Ghouls pretty much handled, Bastian and I got to work on the waiting lycanthropes. Bastian lobbed electricity balls at the dogs, breaking them out of whatever holding pattern they were in. At once, the dogs began their assault, a sure sign that things were not going our way. No pack was this coordinated.

In a heartbeat, my whip was out, the ribbon of death wrapping around one head after the other as it cut through their flesh just as easily as the ghouls. But as awesome as it was, it wasn't working fast enough for my taste. I pulled my gun, hoping the bullets were either silver or at least spelled to do some serious damage. Whip in my right hand and gun in my left, I began firing, the sound like teeny puffs of air rather than blasts of a gun. I wasn't too keen on trying to figure out why my gun sounded like it had a silencer on it, I was just glad someone wasn't going to hear our battle and call the cops.

A ball of fire sailed over my head as the lycanthrope closest to me nearly sank its teeth into my upper arm. The ball exploded against the dog's face, sending embers flying and the lycanthrope rearing back as it clawed at its charring mug. Flames bloomed over its fur, trailing like fingers over its body as the inferno consumed it.

"Move, move, move!" Harper boomed through my earpiece. "Ghouls and lycanthropes are swarming the factory. Get in and get Simon out."

I looked back at the group still fighting and worried if we left them, they'd get killed. But I realized quickly that I didn't have a choice on whether or not I was going to the factory because Bastian scooped me up in his arms and hauled ass to the building ledge. Sailing over the side of the building, I saw a horde of ghouls' racing toward the ground floor bay doors.

Shit, fuck, and damn.

Bastian landed on a metal fire escape and shoved me up the stairs as I tucked the whip and gun back in their holsters. I bounded up the steps as fast as I could, heading for the third-floor catwalk. I grabbed Bastian's hand, yanking him behind me as I picked through booby traps and homemade land mines to the crawlspace above the catwalk.

Paper mills weren't the nicest smelling places, and even though the factory had been decommissioned decades ago, it still had the vague odor of pressed paper. I chose this place because of it, because no matter who followed me home, they would have trouble discerning my scent over the pall of a century's worth of manufactured paper seeping from the walls. But my nose was attuned to the differences in scents, the miasma of chemicals not affecting my nose as it did many other arcaners.

Which was why I shoved Bastian aside as a sword came for our faces once we'd emerged from the crawlspace. The pair of us fell against the rickety safety rail that stopped us from sailing over the side. The metal railing was missing in large chunks, and we were damn lucky to hit a sturdy piece. The sword struck again, and I barely managed to swerve as it came for us. I never figured Booth for a sword man, but he maneuvered the steel like he was born to it, his next strike coming swiftly after his first had missed.

Bastian tossed an electricity ball his way, the shot going wide and exploding against the peeling wall. But even though it didn't hit his target, Booth still ducked, a pause I needed. I yanked my gun and whip free of their holsters, flinging the spelled ribbon out toward Booth. He ducked right where I wanted him to, landing right in my crosshairs as I fired the gun.

But Booth was fast—faster than a bullet—and he moved to the side, the shot hitting him in the shoulder instead of the chest. He staggered back, white fur erupting over his skin, but the shift didn't take him completely.

Bastian moved in front of me, another electricity ball in his hand. "I want you to tell me why. We're your family. We were your pack. You told me as much yourself. You've been with us for half a fucking century, Booth. Why would you take him from me?"

Booth shuddered, his blue eyes glowing bright as he quaked, the phase hitting him hard. "Must take the stealer. He wants her for his own," he growled through his misshapen jaw, the change slowly morphing his features as fur bloomed over his skin. "Must deliver the stealer."

I could only assume the "stealer" was me. I had to say, I was not a fan of the whole "stealer" moniker. Couldn't we come up with a better name that didn't make me sound like the grim fucking reaper?

Yes, this was what I was thinking of instead of realizing that he didn't sound right—not that anyone could sound exactly sane while transforming into a four-legged creature. He sounded like his mind wasn't his own, the monotone making his voice dead. And I was filled with worry about his state of mind, worry about his safety right up until Booth's face morphed into a familiar feline shape.

A shape that tore the last vestige of my family from me.

A shape that murdered Julie.

Booth was the big cat, the white feline with the giant paws that spilled her blood. That took her life.

It was one thing to consider a possibility and quite another to be proven right. Simon's note to *Beware of Booth* was only so poignant out of context. But there was no way to misinterpret this.

My scream of rage and pain could probably be heard for a full city block, and I did not give that first fuck.

"*You.*" I aimed my gun smack-dab in the middle of his forehead. "You took her from me. Why?"

Booth's transformation was completed before my very eyes so I knew he couldn't answer me, but I was *so* tempted to put a bullet in his head and be done with it. Bastian grabbed my wrist, urging me to lower the gun. He couldn't make me. Out of the two of us, I was the stronger one, but I let him push the gun to my side.

"He killed her. He tore her apart," I whispered, the

pain of her death rearing up to bite me.

Bastian wrapped a hand around my middle and set me to the side, putting himself between me and the bastard shifter. "I know, but you can't kill him," he muttered, eyeing the giant feline as he rounded the last corner of his shift.

I met Bastian's gaze with a "wanna bet?" expression on my face.

"I don't think any of them know what they're doing. This is bigger than just Booth. We need him alive if we want to know what happened to Julie and why. We need him to find out what happened to your parents."

Bastian walked over to the giant cat before he could get his bearings and punched him right in the temple, knocking Booth the fuck out. Fur melted away from his face almost instantly as Bastian stepped over him.

"Fun fact," he said over his shoulder as he made his way down the walk, "shifters can't sustain their animal form when they're unconscious."

With Bastian's back turned I was sorely tempted to lop Booth's head right off, but only managed to refrain when I heard the call for help down the catwalk. Growling, I booked it down the grated metal path, to find Bastian in a standoff with two ghouls between him and his brother. Simon was unconscious in a wooden chair, precariously balanced on the edge of the catwalk at one of the spots where the guardrail was missing. Blood trailed down his cheek, spilling onto his flannel shirt, his hands tied to the arms of the chair and a rope around his neck and feet. The rope trailed to a rusted-out pulley with the tail end in one of the ghoul's hands.

And beneath us was nothing but air over an open factory floor.

Heavy metal grating echoed through the open factory, the sound of a multitude of booted feet running toward us made a shiver of fear snake its way up my spine. We didn't have the luxury of time.

Peering through the grated floor, I witnessed Emrys' blazing power shove ghouls to their knees as Thomas' swords cut through their necks at a blurring speed. Axel wielded what appeared to be a Morningstar, bashing anything he could reach. Shouts of spells and incantations echoed off the walls. A great big boom sizzled through the air and ghouls went flying back from a very pissed-off Dahlia as she cut a swath through the swarm, the ripping snarl of battle echoing through the factory.

Even with backup, we were out of time.

As soon as Bastian sensed me behind him, he attacked, orbs of fire and electricity flying in the air as I struck out with my whip, severing the first ghoul's head in a snap. I should have gone for the arm that held onto the rope, but dead seemed better than incapacitated.

I was also incorrect in thinking there were only two ghouls up here. As soon as I lashed out with my whip, two more ghouls dropped from the scant rafters. One landed right behind me and the other next to Simon, jostling his chair closer to the edge of the catwalk.

The ghoul behind me banded his giant arms around the top of my shoulders, hauling me back, dragging me away from the fight. I kicked out, trying to get enough momentum to throw him over my back, but the guy was too big. I tried shooting his feet, but his steps were too fast. Even my attempts at kicking his knees did nothing. In my panic, I forgot the one weapon no one could steal from me.

My teeth.

In a flash of inspiration, I latched my fangs onto the ghoul's forearm, burying the sharp incisors into his flesh. He howled in response, but he was mine now. I took a giant pull of his blood, taking his sin for my own. But by my second pull, I knew the problem. This ghoul —this guy—wasn't a monster.

He was spelled.

His blood showed me a nameless, faceless man, a hooded figure as blurry as a dream. The man was a sorcerer or a mage maybe? Or maybe he was something else. Something older, darker, and far more powerful. The ghoul—Martin—had been a morgue attendant, taking what wouldn't be missed when a body went for cremation. He'd never killed a soul in his entire long life until he'd seen an odd purple light two weeks ago.

This ghoul wasn't responsible for his actions, and I could not end his life—not and value my own.

I ripped my fangs from Martin's arm before using his loose grip to my advantage. In a move I'd used many times before, the giant man was up and over my hip, and with a quick twist of his neck, he was incapacitated. A ghoul could survive a broken neck, easy-peasy.

That was a lesson I learned the hard way.

"Don't kill them," I shouted, racing back to Bastian and Simon.

Bastian's fight with the other ghoul was getting closer and closer to Simon, his chair on the razor's edge of toppling over the side. Simon was slowly regaining consciousness, his head lolling as he tried to focus, his glasses askew on his face.

Then there was a flash of white racing passed my feet. A skeleton cat zipped through stomping feet and leapt, landing on Simon's lap. Isis reached up, raking her claws against Simon's non-bloody cheek, waking him up in earnest.

It took less than a second for Simon to focus on the tableau in front of him and the precarious situation he was in. And still I ran, racing toward Bastian and Simon.

Raising my gun, I aimed for the ghoul that was so close to knocking Simon off into the wide-open nothing, sending up a last-ditch prayer that the damn man didn't fall wrong.

"Bastian, duck!" I yelled, giving him less than a second to comply before I fired.

The bullet seemed to take an age as it crossed the scant space to its target, ripping into the neck of the ghoul, making him stagger. He swayed closer to Simon, his leg knocking into the precariously balanced chair. And then everything slowed to a crawl.

Everything it seemed, except for Bastian.

Bastian's whole body glowed with a silver light, great swirls of white tendrils surrounded his body as he reached for his brother faster than Thomas had ever moved. His fingers closed over the ropes at Simon's wrist, latching onto him with a single-minded focus of a determined man. Then the world snapped back, Bastian's magic failing, but still he held onto Simon.

But Simon was still going down, and if I didn't do something, they would both fall over the ledge. I dove for Simon as I tossed the tail of the whip, praying it wrapped around the above support strut in enough time and didn't slice through metal with the same efficiency as it had ghoul necks.

I sailed over the edge, reaching for the brothers'

joined hands. By some miracle, I latched onto the rope holding Simon to the chair and pulled them with me as we landed in an inelegant pile on the catwalk.

Shaking, I crawled away from the brothers, the act of nearly plummeting to my—well, not *death* but I sure as shit would want it to be.

"A little help down here!" Dahlia called, blasting a rather enormous ghoul right in the face with an orb of magic.

Simon stared at the sea of ghouls and closed his eyes, when he opened them again, his green eyes were all black from pupil to sclera—there was nothing. Then his hands lit with glowing purple magic, the swirls threaded through with inky black. He seemed to pull light and air into himself, the glow of the moon itself dimming. Then all at once, the ghouls fell, crumpling to the ground right where they stood as if they were automatons that had been shut off.

Simon closed his eyes, and then it was like someone plugged the moon back in. Light bloomed through the glass roof once more. Simon's eyes cleared as his magic died, and he looked at his brother.

"How much trouble do you think I'm in?"

And that's when Bastian started laughing.

25

As it turned out, Simon wasn't in too much trouble. Or at least that's what Agents La Roux and Kenzari told us when we delivered a bound and gagged Booth to them on the steps of the Knoxville ABI building. Agent La Roux was tall and scruffy, his black eyes and hair making him look Italian or maybe French, but his accent spoke of snooty boarding schools. Agent Kenzari was a bronze-skinned pixie of a woman, with chin-length black hair and a stare that saw far too much.

She kept staring at me, and I tried to look anywhere else but in her direction, pretending to inspect the ABI building instead of meeting her piercing gaze.

After reading Booth's blood, I learned a frightening number of things about the Night Watch's resident shifter. First, he had most definitely been the shifter that killed Julie and mauled a string of humans. Spelled or not, I still had a frightening urge to kill him, even after the reading. In his memories I saw the same hooded figure that was in the ghoul, Martin's, with the same odd purple glow. There were other sins, some that made me want to rip his soul from his body and watch him crumble to ash, but I refrained.

Still, I was hesitant to deliver him to the ABI, especially if he planned on spilling the beans about the "stealer" he was sent to find, but Bastian and Emrys convinced me to see their side. Booth had mauled humans and killed a venerated oracle. Plus, he'd kidnapped Simon. If we wanted to keep Simon out of hot water, we'd have to put Booth in it.

It helped that Booth was a babbling mess of nonsense once he'd woken up after the read, his words not forming anything intelligible other than the word "ex" repeated over and over again. Either the hooded man fried his brain, or I had, and the fact that I didn't know did not sit well with me.

Neither did the lives we took.

I wondered if all the ghouls we killed were like Martin, good men plucked from their lives to do someone else's bidding. I hated that I didn't know that, either.

Dawn had come and gone sometime in the last few hours and sitting on the steps in the overcast winter morning was not my favorite pastime. I could barely hold my eyes open as Bastian and Agent La Roux processed paperwork, no one wanting to go inside the building for fear of the "Red Queen's wrath." Another pair of agents scooped up Booth, dragging him inside for questioning. I doubted they'd get anything out of him, and I was kind of sorry about that.

Or I would be if him blabbing didn't mean my death.

Soon, I'd have to figure out a place to stay. It wasn't like I could go back to the paper factory after the recent blow-out. By the time we'd left, there were cop cars heading right for it. If they didn't pilfer what I had stashed there, then someone was going to be watching the place. It wasn't safe.

Agent Kenzari sat next to me on the steps, her piercing gaze practically boring a hole in the side of my face.

"How can I help you, Agent?" I asked, my voice as weary as I felt.

Please leave me alone. Pretty please with sugar on top?

"You can call me Sarina if you want," she chirped, far too perky for this time of day. "You're new, aren't you? You can't be more than what? Twenty-two?"

I sighed. *Small talk it was.* "Twenty-three."

"And you've only been undead for a year? It's impressive you can stay awake. Most new vampires are dead to the world around this time of morning."

If I weren't about to pass out from exhaustion, I would have picked up on her leading questions, but I was just too tired. Instead, I yawned. "Just lucky I guess."

"Can I give you a little tip for the future? Just us girls?" she asked, bumping me with her shoulder.

"Fire away," I muttered, resting my cheek on my propped fist, trying to turn my rigid fingers into a suitable pillow.

"If you want to pass as a vamp, you really should wear some contacts. Those purple eyes are striking, but for the old agents—the ones who know a thing or two—they're a dead giveaway."

Said purple eyes flashed open, and I slowly turned my head to look at the perky agent. "You don't say."

She pointed to her head. "I see lots of things, and from what I see, you are a good person. You do good whenever you can, and that is the only reason I'm helping you. Actually, you remind me of a very dear friend. She's a lot like you—a mix of two lines that are far too powerful."

"I don't know—"

"You're not meant to." She cut me off before she

smiled at me, a beatific stretch to her lips that spoke of happiness and contentment, even though her next words were anything but. "We'll need people like you in this world soon enough. Need the strong ones of the old lines to keep this world turning. You're one of the good ones, Sloane. I want you to remember that."

With that, she stood, walking back to La Roux and Bastian as if she hadn't just blown apart my fragile little mind.

Soon, Bastian came back down the stairs, a slew of papers in his hand and an envelope. I figured this was where we parted ways, and I kind of wanted to avoid it.

Rather than waiting for him to tell me I wasn't welcome, I stood, and began heading in the opposite direction of the SUV parked at the curb.

"You're headed in the wrong direction," he called, but I kept walking, picking up my pace and wishing I had a coat against the bitter wind.

Funny, I hadn't felt it before, but now I did.

A moment later, the SUV rolled to a stop next to me, and Bastian got out of the passenger side. Gently, he grabbed my wrist, pulling me to a stop. "I said 'you're headed in the wrong direction.' The car is right here, and it's headed to a place with food and friends and a bed and a roof. It's also headed to a place full of apologies. You didn't deserve the shit we shoved your way. You didn't deserve us doubting you."

He was right, but he was wrong, too.

"I didn't tell you—"

"That was none of my business. We all have secrets, Sloane. I judged you unfairly, and I can promise it will never happen again. You saved my brother's life—even when we treated you like dirt." He shook his head, his expression rueful as he shoved his hands in his pockets. "I owe you more than I can say."

I shivered against the cold, the appeal of a roof over my head almost too good to pass up. Then Julie's vision streaked across my mind. "People are going to be looking for me. I can't—"

Bastian wrapped a blissfully warm arm around my shoulders, effectively cutting off my protest. "Emrys says she has a plan, and when Emrys has a plan, it's best we listen. She'll figure it out." He turned us, steering me toward the passenger seat. "And I'd feel better if you were under a ward, in a place with a lot of people that have more magic than the government deems prudent."

I couldn't really argue with that logic.

"Plus," he murmured in my ear as he opened my door for me, "eventually, I would like to kiss you again, and I can't really do that if I can't find you. It took far too long to locate you the last time."

I stared up at him, mouth agape for a split second before my brain reengaged. "Who says I'd let you?"

Bastian's grin grew wide, rivaling any dastardly smile Thomas had up his sleeve. "I will take that as a personal challenge, Ms. Cabot. Let the games begin."

There was no game playing on the ride home for which I was supremely grateful. I did, however, use Bastian as a pillow and he didn't bitch once, even though Isis was curled in my lap. Simon's cat was stuck to me like glue and had been anytime I was in her general vicinity. I figured it was because I'd saved her human, but with a reanimated skeleton kitty, one never knew.

As soon as we made it back to the house, I trudged up the stairs, intent on a shower and to sleep for about a year. I wasn't particularly settled, nor did I understand all that had transpired over the last few hours, but I couldn't think about those things when I was about to fall off my feet.

Half asleep, I managed to strip, shower, and towel off before falling—literally—into bed. A crinkle of a paper scratched against my face, and I pulled away from the pillow to look at it.

It was a handwritten note, the paper heavy, the scrawl loopy. It took a minute for my eyes to focus enough to read it, the cursive running together, but when I did, I was up and out of bed, backing away from that little slip of paper like it was a damn snake.

I still remember the scent of your parents' skin as they burned. We'll meet again, little one.

—*X*

Booth wasn't saying the word "ex." He was telling me the bastard's name. Booth had somehow known who he was, and he'd managed to hide it from me. Trembling, I sat at the drafting table and stared at the cream note.

So much for feeling safe.

Sloane's story will continue with
Death Watch
Soul Reader Book Two

Are you ready for a new adventure?
Don't miss **Spells & Slip-ups!**
Available on your favorite retailer!

DEATH WATCH

Soul Reader Book Two

A prison break, a secret admirer, and a boatload of lies.

Just about everything Sloane Cabot knows about her past is a big old pile of malarkey. Couple that with the blank spot of how her family died, and she needs answers, like, yesterday.

But when a man shows up dead on her family's grave, she knows it somehow has to be tied to that fateful night a year ago.

Too bad you can't question the dead... *or can you?*

Grab Death Watch today!

DEAD AND GONE
Grave Talker Book Two

There are few things worse than being on the Arcane Bureau of Investigation's naughty list.

To keep herself out of hot water, Darby Adler has made a deal with the devil--using her skills as a grave talker to help the ABI solve some very cold cases.

But there is something mighty amiss in this task--especially when quite a few of these cases lead Darby

right back to her home town of Haunted Peak and the
secrets buried there.

Grab Dead & Gone on Amazon today!

THE ROGUE ETHEREAL SERIES

an adult urban fantasy series by Annie Anderson

Enjoy the Grave Talker Series?
Then you'll love Max!

Come meet Max. She's brash. She's inked. She has a bad habit of dying... *a lot.* She's also a Rogue with a demon on her tail and not much backup.
This witch has a serious bone to pick.

Check out the Rogue Ethereal Series today!

EXCLUSIVE SNEAK PEEKS,
GIVEAWAYS, BOOK DISCUSSION.
COME FOR THE BOOKS.
STAY FOR THE MEMES.

To stay up to date on all things Annie Anderson, get exclusive access to ARCs and giveaways, and be a member of a fun, positive, drama-free space, join The Legion!

ABOUT THE AUTHOR

 Annie Anderson is the author of the international bestselling Rogue Ethereal series. A United States Air Force veteran, Annie pens fast-paced Urban Fantasy novels filled with strong, snarky heroines and a boatload of magic. When she takes a break from writing, she can be found binge-watching The Magicians, flirting with her husband, wrangling children, or bribing her cantankerous dogs to go on a walk.

To find out more about Annie and her books, visit www.annieande.com